The Drummer Boy of Vicksburg

Also by G. Clifton Wisler

G. CLIFTON WISLER

The Drummer Boy of Vicksburg

LODESTAR BOOKS
Dutton   New York

especially for Lilli

Library of Congress Cataloging-in-Publication Data

Wisler, G. Clifton.
    The drummer boy of Vicksburg / G. Clifton Wisler.—1st ed.
        p.   cm.
    Summary: In this fact-based story, fourteen-year-old drummer boy Orion
Howe displays great bravery during a Civil War battle at Vicksburg,
Mississippi.
    ISBN 0-525-67537-X (alk. paper)
    1. Howe, Orion P., d. 1930—Juvenile fiction.   2. United States—History—
Civil War, 1861–1865—Juvenile fiction.   [1. Howe, Orion P., d. 1930—
Fiction.   2. United   States—History—Civil   War,   1861–1865—Fiction.
3. Heroes—Fiction.]   I. Title.
PZ7.W78033Dr   1997
[Fic]—dc20   96-21184   CIP   AC

Published in the United States by Lodestar Books,
an affiliate of Dutton Children's Books,
a member of Penguin Putnam Inc.,
375 Hudson Street, New York, New York 10014

Published simultaneously in Canada
by McClelland & Stewart, Toronto

Editor: Rosemary Brosnan   Designer: Dick Granald

Printed in the U.S.A.   First Edition   10   9   8   7   6   5   4   3   2

Colonel Oscar Malmborg (left) with Orion P. Howe

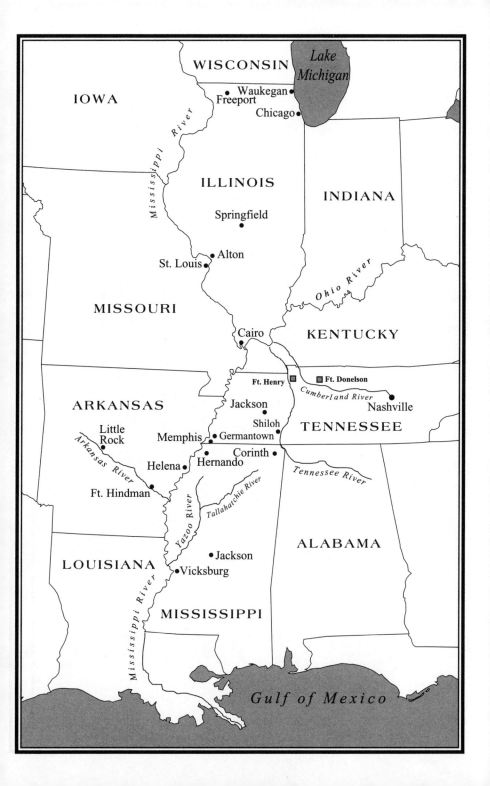

Roll of the Fifty-fifth Illinois Infantry Regiment

Union Department of the Tennessee

COMMANDER
Maj. Gen. Ulysses S. Grant

FIFTEENTH ARMY CORPS
Maj. Gen. Willliam T. Sherman

SECOND DIVISION
Maj. Gen. Frank P. Blair (replaced Morgan L. Smith)

SECOND BRIGADE
Col. Thomas K. Smith

FIFTY-FIFTH ILLINOIS INFANTRY REGIMENT
Col. David Stuart (1861–62)
Col. Oscar Malmborg (1862–64)

STAFF
Edward O. F. Roler, regimental surgeon
Captain Milton L. Haney, chaplain
William H. Howe, fife major

MUSICIANS
Lyston D. Howe, company B
Joseph W. Edwards, company I

(Union regiments originally contained ten companies of
approximately 100 men each.)

COMPANY C
Commander: Captain Francis H. Shaw
Sergeant John Curtiss
Corporal Michael Ainsbury
Corporal Jim Frazier
Privates: Orin Babcock, Rienzi Cleveland,
George Crowell, Henry Curtiss, Robert Hamer,
Philip Pitts, Henry Woodring, and others.
Drummer: Orion Howe

 ONE

I never considered myself a hero. I led no charge, and I captured no battle flag. The truth is, I didn't make the best sort of soldier. I was usually in the wrong place at the wrong time, or else I was doing the wrong thing. I didn't join up after hearing some senator or Methodist preacher inspire the population. I didn't sign a muster book with my folks and friends cheering. I joined no parade of boyhood pals, and I won no kisses from the pretty girls. In fact, I don't think anyone wanted me in the army in the first place, and it was mostly by accident that I ended up there.

It all began with the drums. Two drums. My pa, Will Howe, bought them for my little brother, Lyston, and me when we were just pups.

"Music's your heritage," Pa told us when he handed over the sticks. "You know I was a musician in the war with Mexico."

We knew that, all right. Whenever anyone came to share Sunday dinner, Pa would entertain them with tales of his army days. To hear him tell it, he practically won the war single-handedly despite passing most of his time in a

1

Michigan hospital. He only got to Mexico because some-body forgot to give him his discharge papers, and he stayed there because he was too stubborn to leave.

"What else could I do?" he told Lyston and me one night when beset by a sudden plague of honesty. "I had no money, no job, no family eager to take me in. I belonged there, with the soldiers. I did them some good."

"How, Pa?" Lyston asked.

"A soldier's mostly cold, hungry, and homesick when he's preparing to fight. He doesn't feel like much. He'd like to stand up and yell, feel brave and powerful, but he's only got his one little voice, and it's hard to be heard amid all the cannons and rifles. The notes from my fife and the beat of the drums gave voice to his feelings. Later, when the night grew cold, I could offer a song from home to warm him. A musician may not blast a fort half so well as a twelve-pounder cannon, but he's important just the same."

That meant something to Pa, being important. Granny Howe said it was on account of him being smallish. Maybe she had a point. Pa stood only five feet four inches high, and Illinoians as a rule ran to tall. If you're a cabinet maker, even a good one, you pass most of your time alone in a shop. You don't have much chance to boast about that. On the other hand, when he took out his fife to play for the local militia or entertain at a political rally, people took notice.

I suppose that Pa hoped the drums would give us the same chance. I think he wanted us to have that feeling of belonging. It was his way of tying us to those better days of his. He wasn't a man to share his deep feelings, to tell us he loved us. The drums spoke for him.

2

Pa was right about music being a heritage. Lyston and I both had a talent for picking up tunes, and it wasn't two weeks before we were drumming up a storm. At first we drummed the old army commands Pa taught us. Later, though, we created our own marches and even made up words to go along. Granny outfitted us in white trousers and little blue uniform tunics, and we played at church picnics, birthday parties, and even political rallies.

People took to us.

"Sometimes I imagine your blessed mother standing on that hillside, watching," Granny declared. "She'd be so proud."

Ma, having died when we were little, had to watch from a higher vantage point. Pa's new wife, Cordelia, didn't share his opinion of our drumming.

"Do you boys have to stir up a ruckus every single time I try to get some rest?" she stormed at us one Saturday.

"Sorry," I said, motioning for Lyston to stop. "We were only practicing."

"Do it somewhere else," she suggested. "The neighbors are complaining."

They were, too. One afternoon Lyston and I led a parade of our schoolmates down Washington Street. While we beat our drums, the other boys balanced brooms on their shoulders. We were a regular little army, and a group of girls slightly older than I was tossed flowers at us. I confess that I was grinning like a fool.

"There go the famous Howes again," Mr. Garner remarked as we passed his house. "Best-known nuisances in Waukegan!"

"You're as welcome as a thousand hungry locusts in a

wheat field, Orion," Mrs. Kruger, the wife of the dairyman, told me later that same day. "My cows are off their feed, and I'm short fifteen gallons of milk this week alone!"

The townsfolk tolerated us for a time. Later on, a sheriff's deputy advised us that drumming sounded better if played closer to the shore of Lake Michigan.

"Maybe your business would do better in Chicago," Mrs. Kruger told Pa.

Being boys, we took the complaints as a declaration of war. They only made us play louder and more often.

The truth was that Pa was right about drumming. It did make you feel tall. By the spring of 1860, when I was eleven and Lyston was nine, we were good at it. That being an election year, Pa arranged for us to bang away at our drums while he played the fife in order to draw crowds to rallies. Mostly we played for candidates for Congress or local folks hoping to talk their way into the legislature. On April 2, though, we played outside Dickinson Hall in downtown Waukegan on behalf of a Springfield politician we would hear a lot about those next few years—Abraham Lincoln.

Local Republicans were split in their views at the time. Most favored either Mr. William Seward of New York or Mr. Simon Cameron of Pennsylvania. Pa told us that this fellow Lincoln was a railroad lawyer who had made his name some years before, debating Senator Stephen Douglas. The "little giant," as Mr. Douglas was called, was the champion of the Democrats, so Mr. Lincoln's opposing him won favor with Illinois Republicans. I was too young to pay attention to politics, but I confess Mr. Lincoln made an impression.

4

First of all, he was tall. He spoke with a slow, south-country accent, and he smiled easily and without pretense. On his way into the hall, he paused and greeted Lyston and me warmly.

"I'm always glad to see young people taking an interest in national affairs," he told me as he gripped my hand. His fingers nearly crushed mine!

I grinned back at him anyway. When Lyston started to speak up, I elbowed him silent.

"I'm more interested in getting paid," he whispered afterward.

"Well, you don't have to tell *him* that," I argued. "You want to be invited back, don't you, L?"

I guess we earned our money that night because the hall was full to overflowing. Mr. Lincoln started his speech with a joke. Then he turned stern and serious, telling us there was no just reason to allow slavery to spread. Well, that brought a cheer from the audience. Even those who weren't openly abolitionist thought that the new territories we won in the war with Mexico ought to be free. Mr. Lincoln resumed his speech, but he broke off in midsentence when the town fire bell sounded outside.

"Fire!" someone in the back hollered. "Fire!"

Half the crowd rose up and stared at the doors, but Mr. E. P. Perry, who had organized the meeting, called for calm.

"Please, ladies and gentlemen, remain seated," he urged. "This is nothing but an attempt by hooligans to silence our speaker."

Mr. Lincoln gazed at the windows, though. There was a reddish glare coming from the waterfront.

"I think there *is* a fire," he announced. "You better go and try to save the property. I can come some other time to speak to you."

Now there was a sensible man! He put fires above words. Before you could shake a stick, people were pouring out the doors and heading down the street. The big Case and Bull warehouse burned that night, but thanks to Mr. Lincoln, long lines of bucket-toting people doused the flames before the rest of the waterfront turned to ashes.

"I've heard of fiery speeches," Pa joked afterward, "but nothing like this."

That summer the newspapers carried stories about the split of the Democrats into Northern and Southern factions. The Republicans, meeting in Chicago, nominated the little-known Lincoln. I regretted that he had not had the chance to finish his speech. It seemed more and more possible that he would be our next president.

"That fool's stirring everyone up!" Jake Grimsley complained one morning as we sat together outside the school building. "Pa says we'll find ourselves fighting a war."

"A war?" I asked. "Why?"

"Because the abolitionists want to free all the slaves," Jake told me. "We've got family down South. They won't abide us interfering with their affairs."

I didn't hold with slavery myself, but I'd learned not to argue about it. I was half a head shorter than Jake, and I wouldn't fare too well in a fight.

"Maybe Mr. Lincoln'll come back and explain it all," Lyston suggested a day or so later. "He's probably got a plan to stop us from having a war."

"Sure," I answered. I didn't much believe it, though.

Waukegan was torn in half by rival groups trying to shout each other down. The Douglas Invincibles, as they called themselves, pushed the Democratic view. They were opposed by the Republicans' Wide Awake Committee.

"Wake up, friends!" they shouted as they marched along in their black caps and long capes. "Rise to the true cause! Free the enslaved! Put an end to the slave power of the South!"

It was the Wide Awakes who invited Pa and us to play for a Lincoln rally in September. It was a big gathering. Dozens of families drove their wagons, rode on horseback, or walked along Sheridan Road to a large grove not far from the shore of Lake Michigan. The Wide Awakes marched in front, holding liberty torches in their hands. Except for the county fairs held at Libertyville, I had never seen anything to match it.

"You'd think a circus was coming to town!" Lyston exclaimed as we watched them pass along the dusty road.

"Does seem that way," I confessed.

"Do you think *he's* coming?" Lyston asked. "Mr. Lincoln? Maybe he'll shake *my* hand this time."

"No," I answered, sighing. "Don't you remember what Pa said? It's just a rally for him, L. Congressman Lovejoy's speaking."

"That abolitionist fellow?" Lyston asked, groaning.

I laughed. Lyston had turned ten in August, but he still didn't have much patience for listening to preachers and such. The Lovejoy brothers, Owen and Elijah, were famous abolitionists. Elijah was dead now, shot years ago when a pro-slavery mob attacked his newspaper.

7

"Before that," Pa told me, "there wasn't much sentiment in Illinois for freeing the slaves. Afterward, abolition parties sprang up all over."

That evening, as Lyston and I beat our drums and led a parade of Waukegan boys toward the lake, I still wasn't sure whether we were siding with the abolitionists, the unionists, or what.

"Seems to me they're all one and the same," Pa remarked once the speeches were over. "Most of us are opposed to those Southern hotheads breaking up the country!"

It wasn't words that I remembered about that night, though. I recalled the wondrous bonfires that lit up the shore and our little band of mock soldiers, each of us wearing a homemade uniform and doing his best to puff himself up. There were whole battalions of pretty girls dressed in white, waving flags and cheering us on. I confess that I put on my best show for them.

As if to answer our drumming and the fiery speeches, thunder began to boom from the far shore of Lake Michigan. I sniffed rain and gazed homeward. The politicians hurried to their carriages, and those who rode horses or arrived in wagons began departing. The rest of us followed.

No Independence Day fireworks ever matched the display the heavens put on that night. Lightning streaked across the sky, illuminating the lakefront. Thunder shook the earth. A wind blew up, and soon raindrops began pelting us.

At first our little band tried to maintain some sense of order, but the arrival of hailstones dissolved our formation into forty fools fleeing wildly toward the refuge of town. Our house being farther away than most, I decided to seek

8

cover instead of spattering my way down Sheridan Road. I grabbed Lyston, and together we scrambled up a small hill and huddled beneath a grove of oaks.

"Look out there," Lyston called, and my eyes followed his pointing finger to the lake. A few hundred feet from shore, a slender boat fought its way toward land. Flames licked at its stern, and people jumped from its decks into the water. Even the downpour failed to dampen the fierce blaze. Soon the entire ship was afire.

"Would you look at that!" someone yelled from the road.

"It's the *Lady Elgin*," another added.

"Steamer," Lyston noted. "Must have hundreds of people aboard."

I cringed at the thought. The wind carried the desperate cries of the passengers to shore. I gasped as one man peeled off his burning shirt and then dove from the bow into the water. Another and another followed.

"Those aren't torches, are they?" Lyston asked as sparkling flickers of reddish yellow fell into the lake.

"No," I muttered. "They're people."

The ship went on burning for half an hour or more before the dark swallowed it. The storm drowned out the last cries. Once the rain ceased, small parties appeared along the shore with torches.

"We should help," Lyston told me.

"What use can two boys be?" I asked. "We're soggy wet, and we've still got our drums. We ought to hurry on home."

"It's better than an hour's walk," he argued. "We can help for a time. Somebody with a wagon's bound to come along, and we can ride with them back to town."

9

It made sense, so we slung our drum sashes over our shoulders and started toward the torchbearers. I wish we hadn't.

I had never in all my life seen anything like it. The charred remains of the *Lady Elgin*'s hulk stood offshore. Little more than the smokepipes and pilothouse remained above water. As for the passengers, only a few had reached shore alive. Three hundred drowned.

By daybreak, when Lyston and I finally climbed into a bakery wagon and headed home, dozens of bodies had drifted ashore. Some were horribly burned, but those weren't the ones that troubled me most. No, it was the ones that just lay there, pale and calm as if they were sleeping, that haunted me. Lyston and I helped drag two boys and a little girl up on the bank.

"I never saw a dead person before," Lyston said as we folded their wrinkled arms across their bare chests.

"I saw Ma," I said, trembling. "But it wasn't like this."

"I never did like boats," Lyston added. "Orry, I don't know which would be worse, drowning or burning up."

"I don't believe I'd care to try either," I said, trying to cheer him up.

"Nor me, neither," he replied. "Orry, do you put much stock in portents?"

"No," I told him. "I know Pa's forever reading omens in this or that, but I figure what's bound to happen will."

"I don't know I agree," he said, staring at the dead children. "There's a lot of talk about us fighting a war with the South if Mr. Lincoln's elected president. You figure we will?"

"No," I said, leading him away from the corpses. "People like to talk big, but they're not altogether crazy. It won't come to war, and even if it did, you wouldn't be in it."

"Sure," he said, leaning against my shoulder.

As it turned out, though, I was wrong on both counts.

 TWO

When we finally got home, Granny chewed our ears for staying out all night. Pa mostly shrugged it off.

"They're not children anymore," he pointed out.

I heard him telling Cordelia that the way things were going, boys our age would be growing up fast those next few years. He was right as rain.

Mr. Lincoln won the presidency handily despite the fact that he wasn't even on the ballot in most Southern states. Even before he took office, South Carolina stirred up a hornet's nest by announcing it was seceding—pulling out of the Union. Down South states began pulling out right and left, seizing federal forts, armories, customs houses, and the like. When the Carolinians tried to take over Fort Sumter in Charleston Harbor in April 1861, the shooting started.

"Will there be a war?" I asked Pa.

"Yes," he told me. "The president's asked for seventy-five thousand troops to put down the rebellion. You don't need that many men to hold a parade. We didn't have nearly so many in Mexico, and they had a well-trained, professional army. By the look of it, son, we're already in a war."

It wasn't long before a couple of fellows came up from Springfield with authority to muster recruits. Pa hurried right down to the enlistment office and volunteered to play his fife. Lyston and I brought our drums out after school, and the three of us, together with some other town boys, formed a sort of recruiting band.

That was my first taste of the army, and it wasn't all that bad. Ladies brought us roast beef and ham for supper, and Miss Charity Spencer even baked us a Dutch apple pie. A few men came by each day, swore the oath, and signed a muster book. Boys only a few grades ahead of me in school arrived, boasting of how they would drive the rebels from the battlefield and restore the Union. You were supposed to be eighteen to enlist, but I knew several who added a year or two to their ages.

While Pa played his fife and directed us, Lyston and I drummed. We started in April, and we kept it up right through May. By then companies were forming regularly and marching along to Chicago or Springfield. The day before Company I of the Fifteenth Illinois Infantry started for Freeport, their captain begged Pa to come along.

"The boys are unsettled," he explained. "Having your little band with us will set them at ease."

Since most of Waukegan's unmarried men and quite a few of the boys, too, had already donned Union blue, Pa agreed to go. For Lyston and me, it seemed like a real adventure. We got to ride the train to Chicago and then west another hundred miles to Freeport. That was where the recruits officially joined the Fifteenth Illinois. All along the way people showed up, waving flags and cheering us. Once we stepped down from the train at Freeport, pretty girls rushed in and kissed the younger soldiers. Their mothers made a fuss over Lyston and me, even though we did our best to attract the girls.

It was hopeless, though. When one pretty young lady of fourteen or so finally walked up and took my hands, it was only because she wanted to meet one of the lieutenants.

"I might be a lieutenant myself," I told her.

"No, you're only a little drummer boy. Not even as cute as your young friend there," she added, pointing to Lyston. "I'll bet they won't even take you with them when they go."

I scowled. You couldn't argue with the truth of her words, but the sentiment was downright depressing. I tried to tell her how Pa said musicians were important, but the lieutenant appeared first. Off she went.

We remained in Freeport a little shy of two weeks, drumming and helping the regiment learn its drill. Then Pa declared business was piling up back home, and we returned to Waukegan. I expected that to be the end of our soldiering, for everyone said the war would be over by Christmas. It didn't work out that way, though.

I knew something was up the day Granny left for Chicago.

"See you soon, dear," she said as she hugged me at the depot.

She gave Lyston a longer, more serious hug. That was peculiar.

Then there was Pa. I never saw him work half as hard at filling orders. He usually slowed down some once winter passed so he could take us fishing or duck hunting along the lake. The first week of June I overheard him arguing with

Cordelia. Then he called for Lyston and me to meet him at the dinner table.

"Boys, I've received a letter," he told us. "The Fifteenth Illinois needs a fife major, and they've offered me the job. All my business is completed here, so I have decided to join the army."

"Oh, Pa, that's a good joke," Lyston said, cackling. "You're too old to go soldiering."

"You know yourselves how these young drummers need an experienced man to take them in hand," Pa growled. "I'm going."

"Then you'll take us along, won't you?" I asked.

"I wouldn't care for you boys to neglect your studies," Pa declared. "Especially you, Orion. You'll want to earn a respectable place in one of the better schools."

"Ah, there's sure to be time for that later," I complained. "A man has his duty to think about. I can—"

"No, I decided that much weeks ago," Pa replied. "Your grandmother's taken rooms in Chicago. You'll go and stay with her and attend school."

"Can I come then?" Lyston asked.

Now that was a foolish question. I was close to four foot eight inches tall and twelve and a half years old. Lyston wasn't yet eleven, and he stood not a scratch taller than four foot two.

"Just the thing I had in mind," Pa said.

I sat there, eyes wide with disbelief, as Lyston whooped and howled with pleasure.

"But Pa," I objected. "What will people think, me staying behind while my little brother joins the army?"

15

"They'll think you have lessons to worry over," he replied.

It was more than a soul could bear! I could just imagine Lyston surrounded by girls, boasting about his battles while I worked math problems and wrote essays. I would be remembered as the Howe who stayed in Chicago while his brother, father, and classmates fought the rebels and saved the Union.

Bad as it seemed at the time, I felt even worse as the weeks went on. Granny enrolled me in a serious school in downtown Chicago. I slaved from dawn to dusk, working difficult problems and trying desperately to catch up with my better-educated classmates. Almost daily one of the older boys left school and joined some new regiment. I envied each and every one of them.

To make matters worse, the war went bad for the Union. The rebs in Virginia whipped General McDowell at a place called Bull Run in July and chased our army back to Washington. In August another rebel army killed General Lyon at Wilson's Creek in Missouri and started north toward St. Louis.

I took that news hard. Pa and Lyston were somewhere in Missouri. It seemed as though the Fifteenth might be the next unit crushed by the South's victorious forces.

Lyston never got far enough south to face the rebs, though. He was young and small, and army life proved too much for him. Pa wrote me how the whole regiment adopted him as a sort of pet. They had to shorten his drum sash to almost nothing to keep the drum from dragging in the dirt, and they carried his other equipment with the surgeon's gear. Even so, marching through the wet, muddy Ozark country brought on fever. He was sick most of August, and in September he took on the additional burden of rheumatism.

Pa was never one to spend a penny without reason. When his telegram arrived at Granny's rooms, I felt an icy chill creep up my spine. It read: *Orion, your brother seriously ill. We arrive Chicago 22 October.*

It was already the twenty-second. I told Granny, and we hired a wagon to take us to the station. The train was late, so we had time after all.

"Orry, I want you to understand something," Granny said as we waited. "Your pa's prone to exaggeration, so don't expect the worst. If Lyston were seriously ill, they wouldn't be traveling."

"Maybe," I said, unconvinced. "He couldn't keep Ma from dying. He found himself a new wife without much trouble. He and Cordelia can have lots of children. So Lyston's not so important to him."

Granny reddened bright as a tomato, and I thought for a moment that she was going to wallop me. I could see her fingers tightening into a ball, and she clamped hold of my shoulder.

"I don't ever want to hear another word along those lines, Orion P. Howe!" she exclaimed. "Whatever else you imagine about your father, you can't believe he doesn't care for his boys. You two are everything to him. If he remarried, it was to provide you with a mother as much as to acquire himself a wife."

"Then why take Lyston into the army?" I asked. "He

17

knew how little L was. Maybe we didn't know marching would wear him down, but Pa did. He was in Mexico, after all."

"He couldn't afford to send both of you to school," Granny explained. "And he knew Lyston could wait a bit."

"We might have stayed in Waukegan."

"You don't get along with Cordelia very well," Granny reminded me.

"I guess it's my fault then," I muttered.

"It's nobody's fault," she insisted. "Most things that happen just happen. The important thing is that your brother's coming home. We've got a real challenge, Orion. We have to cheer him and heal him."

"Don't worry," I said, forcing a smile to my lips. "We'll do it."

I meant that, too. L and I were close, and if it was in my power to make him well, I would. I wasn't prepared for the sight of that train, though. It was full of sick and wounded soldiers, many of them just boys. Some hobbled down from the cars on crutches. As many as half of them displayed empty sleeves or trouser legs. I watched one poor boy who couldn't have been more than sixteen try to hug his mother with the stumps of two arms.

Lyston didn't walk from the train. Instead, an orderly helped Pa carry Lyston's stretcher. L was pitifully pale and even thinner than when he'd left. He managed to grin at Granny, and he lifted his head a little when I clasped his hand.

"Here," the orderly said after helping to load Lyston in the back of our wagon. "Don't lose these."

18

"What?" I asked as he stuffed some thin sheets of paper into my pocket.

"His discharge papers," the orderly explained. "Present them to the quartermaster, and they'll bury him for free."

"Nobody's burying anybody!" Pa shouted. "Certainly not that boy there."

"They don't let 'em out unless it's hopeless," the orderly argued. "Might as well prepare yourselves."

Granny started to reply, but Lyston coughed, and she climbed up beside him instead. I was already there. As soon as Pa joined us, she urged the driver to take us home.

The army might have given up on Lyston, but they didn't know the Howes. A few days of Granny's cooking; a clean, dry bed; and a chapter of Charles Dickens each night brought Lyston back from the grave. He took on weight, and in a week, he was walking around, making himself a nuisance.

By then Pa had headed along to Waukegan to see Cordelia and tend to some business. He only had a twenty-day furlough, not a discharge like Lyston.

"Look after your brother," he told me when I walked him to the station. "Mind your studies, too."

"Yes, sir," I promised.

It was only after Pa left that Lyston would tell me much about his time in the army.

"It's a hard life, soldiering," L told me. "It seems like you're forever drilling or marching. Drummers have to beat out this call or that, announcing everything from breakfast to supper and a dozen other things as well."

"From the look of those boys at the station," I said, "you had some fierce fights down in Missouri."

"I suppose," he grumbled. "I wasn't in any. Before we got very far south, I took sick."

"Pa should've seen to it that they didn't overwork you," I argued.

"Oh, half the regiment was sick at one time or another, Orry. It wasn't Pa's fault. I was pretty small for a drummer."

"Pa wrote how they shortened your straps."

"Yeah," he said, nodding. "The rain and the cold took their toll, and the food was awful. Nobody in the Fifteenth could cook. We got moldy flour, and the meat was worse. I wish they could have spared us from drill a day or two. We could have fished the creeks."

"Well, you're better now. Maybe we can find you a school."

"Oh, I'm not through with the army," Lyston announced. "Soon as I'm well enough, I'm going to find me a new regiment. Now I know the calls, I'll be more use."

"L, that's crazy!" I cried.

"No, it seems sensible enough. I can't very well sit in a classroom when there's a war going on."

I sighed.

"Orry, I'm not saying you shouldn't."

"Granny'll have a fit!"

"And how do you feel about it?"

"I think you ought to stay here through winter. You were always quick to take a chill."

"I won't wait too long."

"You won't do the army much good dead," I scolded. "Besides, Pa might let me go with you. We'd do better, the pair of us."

"Maybe," he replied. "At least you can fry an egg and boil sausages."

"I'm glad you missed me, L."

"I did, too," he said, laughing. "I still don't know how to sew. Up in the Ozarks I ripped my pants, and I was a week finding somebody to stitch them proper."

"Sounds to me like you ought to talk Granny into joining up with you. You only want me to sew and cook."

"You spin a fair yarn, Orry," Lyston said, laughing. "You'd be wonderful help pranking the sergeants, too. Besides, Granny wouldn't come."

I punched his arm lightly, and he pretended to be hurt. Granny looked in on us and laughed.

"Behave yourselves!" she said. "I've still got a peach switch set aside to wallop a boy or two with."

"No need," Lyston assured her. "We were only pretending."

"Just don't pretend your way into trouble, young men," she added. "Now, get ready for supper. Orion, are your lessons finished?"

"Yes, ma'am," I said, sighing. They weren't, but if I confessed it, she would have had me at them half the night. I had another chapter of Dickens to read Lyston, and I still hadn't heard all his war stories.

 THREE

Between L's stories and the worsening news from the battlefields, I found it harder then ever to concentrate on my studies. It didn't seem to matter very much how long it took a train to go from Baltimore to Chicago or which Roman emperor was which. School was losing its hold on everyone. The older boys were all gone by November. Most of the faculty left, too. Only gray-haired old men and preachers remained to teach us.

Once Lyston got back on his feet, we began passing our afternoons watching new recruits drill down by the lake. The army had constructed a line of rough-cut barracks across some sandy knolls near the university. They named the place Camp Douglas, after the "little giant." Senator Douglas, having lost the election, had done his best to keep his Southern supporters in the Union. He made speeches all over the place, but nothing helped. The travel broke his health, and he died of a fever. Granny said it was more likely from a broken heart.

A Chicago lawyer, David Stuart, was arranging a whole

brigade of troops to honor the senator. As men marched in from the countryside, Stuart formed them into regiments. They were mostly country boys, although some were from the bigger towns of northern Illinois. Those boys were a far cry from soldiers, though. Only a few officers boasted uniforms, and the men used broom handles as they practiced their musket drill. The day Lyston and I appeared with our drums and homemade uniforms, they greeted us with open arms.

"These two appear to know their business," a fair-haired fellow announced. "You boys looking for a regiment to join?"

"No," I answered. "Just thought we might beat our drums."

"Couldn't hurt," the soldier declared. "Name's Jim Frazier, from Durand up in Winnebago County."

"Orion Howe," I said, clasping his hand. "This is my brother, Lyston. He's a veteran of the Missouri fighting."

"Must have been hard fighting," Jim said, smiling. "Wore the poor boy right down to a nub."

Lyston tried to pretend anger, but those fellows were such a cheerful lot that it couldn't be sustained. We drummed for their drill that afternoon and were invited back. It wasn't long before they got their uniforms, boots, and belts. The drill improved. As for muskets, they would have to wait a while longer.

In the days that followed, L and I sort of loaned ourselves to what became the Fifty-fifth Illinois Infantry regiment. Each company had its own regular drummer, and together they made up a little band. Lyston and I did our best to tutor

23

the drummers, teaching them the military calls and all. Not many boys, or men, either, will take instruction from a pair of half-pints, though. What they needed was a fife major, and guess who they got? Pa!

I never was sure exactly how Pa arranged it, but he managed to get transferred from the Fifteenth to the Fifty-fifth and then get himself promoted to fife major, or principal musician, as he liked to call it. That left him in charge of the ten drummers and ten fifers. He instructed them in their duties, but otherwise he left them alone. Our little band quickly became a source of amusement to the soldiers and of torment to the officers.

By that time Pa had taken on the unofficial name of "Waukegan." Nobody faulted him for doing his job, but more than a few of the younger men laughed at the way he pranced around, stretching his five feet four inches into Napoleonic exaggeration. L and I were soon dubbed "Waukegan's pups." We tried to take it good-naturedly, but it wasn't always easy. One afternoon Henry Woodring, a six-footer from Rockford, threw a burlap bag over my head and dragged me off into the scrub oak that lined the camp.

"Between the lieutenant colonel and your papa, we've got about all the sawed-off soldiers a regiment can abide," he grumbled as he tied me to an oak.

Well, it didn't take me long to wiggle out of the ropes and free myself. By then my face was red as a beet, and my dander was up. Woodring might have been a foot and a half taller and double my age, but I was prepared to do him damage. I raced back toward the Fifty-fifth's camp, but before I could do myself any harm, Jim Frazier and Little Joe Edwards, Company I's drummer, grabbed me.

24

"I know it's a sorry trick to play on anyone, bagging them," Jim admitted, "but he's too big to fight."

"Not fair anyhow," Joe added.

Now Joe was a downright scamp. No nice way to put it. He was no bigger than Pa, skinny as a rail, and never shy about sassing anybody. He boasted he was twenty-one, but I always judged him considerably younger. His uncle was colonel of the Fortieth Illinois, and if Joe had been eighteen, I suspect he would have joined up with him. I figured that a third of the Fifty-fifth was underage, so nobody in his company was going to ask questions.

"There's all kinds of fighting back," Joe told me. "We runts don't stand much of a chance toe-to-toe with a giant like Woodring. You have to find his weak spot, slither over, and wham!"

It sounded easier than it was. Woodring may not have been long on tolerating drummers, but he was careful about his duties. He prided himself on keeping his boots shined and his uniform straight. He even took the trouble to wash regularly. That proved his undoing. I bided my time two whole days. Then, with Joe's help, I sneaked up to where Woodring and a half dozen others were taking turns washing in a heated tub. Joe snatched the big private's shirt, and I got his trousers. With the aid of one of Granny's knitting needles, I managed to break the stitches along both shoulders and the seat of his pants. It would have taken a careful glance to see because I didn't rip out the threads. So Henry Woodring was as surprised as anybody when his uniform came apart during dress parade. There he stood, all six feet of him, bare save for flannel drawers! The whole regiment broke out laughing.

25

Except, that is, for Henry Woodring and Lieutenant Colonel Malmborg. The colonel, who took parade seriously, pounded his boot on the earth and shouted a mixture of Swedish and English curses.

"Woodring, get your uniform in order before Colonel Malmborg dies of apoplexy," Captain Shaw urged.

Woodring grabbed his shredded uniform and raced away. The regiment straightened its lines and continued the parade. The music was a little ragged, though, because Joe Edwards and I were cackling like hens.

I learned a rare truth the next day when Henry Woodring lifted me onto his shoulder and carried me through camp.

"You'll do, Howe," he told me. "I wouldn't tolerate a man or boy either one who'd fail to avenge a torment."

"So, what are you planning to do with me?" I asked, not a little nervous.

"Well, I could dump you in Lake Michigan and see if you can swim," he said. "Or—"

"Or what?" I asked.

"Make you my friend," he said, offering his hand.

"I like the second choice better," I told him.

"Me, too," he said. "I was up half the night sewing."

Gradually the Fifty-fifth took on the appearance of a fighting regiment. This was mainly due to the efforts of Lieutenant Colonel Malmborg. He wasn't the most likable man, but he knew his business. The colonel had attended a military school in Sweden. Like Pa, he was a veteran of the Mexican War.

It was nevertheless amusing to see him put the men through their drill. He had a harsh sort of accent that hardened his words and often twisted them as well.

"Column py file!" he would bark, and the men would change formation.

Sometimes, when he was particularly excited, his words would simply unravel.

"Charge pea-nets mit!" he ordered once. Now there wasn't a bayonet in the whole regiment anyway, but the notion of charging with pea-nets, or peanuts, as Joe suggested, was too much for even the solemn-faced Captain Shaw. He bent over, laughing.

On December 9, the day I dreaded most arrived. The Fifty-fifth lined up with several other regiments and began marching triumphantly down Michigan Avenue. Handkerchiefs fluttered from the windows of buildings on either side of the street, and it seemed as if ten thousand people cheered us on. Once we reached the Chicago and Alton Railroad Station, Lyston and I gazed up hopefully at Pa.

"We trained with these men," I argued. "We ought to go along."

"At least as far as Saint Louis," L added.

"Boys, we've got our full complement of musicians," Pa explained. "You've neglected your studies long enough. Winter's sure to be here any day, and campaigning is hard on boys. You know that, Lyston."

"Maybe we can join you in the spring then?" L asked.

"God willing, the war will be over by then," Pa said, pulling us to his sides. "I'm proud of you both. Now go and join your grandmother. She's waiting to take you home."

The war didn't end quickly, though. I read the disappointment in Pa's letters. The regiment missed the great victories at Forts Henry and Donelson because the guns issued them at St. Louis proved worthless. I knew how bitter a pill that would be for my friends to swallow, especially when Pa wrote how nearly a fifth of the thousand soldiers who had mustered at Camp Douglas were too sick to continue in service. Some had already died.

The worst blow of all followed. I returned from school one afternoon in February to find Lyston gone.

"He's returned to the army," Granny said as she passed a letter into my hands. Company B's drummer was sick, and Pa had sent for L.

Your brother has the experience, Pa wrote. *Devote yourself to your studies, Orion. Your time may come before this awful war is over.*

I doubted that. The newspapers were full of rebel defeats. General U. S. Grant, the victor at Forts Henry and Donelson, was driving the secessionists out of Tennessee. We were making our way down the Mississippi River. The navy was blockading Southern ports, and a new general, George McClellan, was moving toward Richmond, Virginia, the rebel capital.

Whether out of genius or desperation, the rebels struck back. At a ferryboat stop on the Tennessee River called Pittsburg Landing, the rebs came within a whisker of destroying Grant's entire army. I was proud when I heard how the Fifty-fifth had fought at the battle the papers dubbed Shiloh, after a small church on the battlefield. My Illinois friends had struggled against great odds, especially the first day, when they fought virtually alone on the far side of the field. Fifty-one of them died, and another two hundred suffered wounds. Within two weeks, thirty-five of those were also dead.

I was relieved when I learned that Pa and L had made it through the fighting without a scratch. L took sick afterward. For three days he lay feverish and near death at the landing. Then he improved.

I read every account of Shiloh carried by the newspapers, but I had no sense of what had happened there. Letters and telegrams had only words, and words alone were not enough. I heard more details about the battle while visiting Camp Douglas, where the rebels captured at Shiloh arrived during the second week of April.

The old camp of instruction had been walled into a prison, and the ragged, dirty rebels who stepped off the Chicago and Alton cars trudged their way there. I just sort of wandered around the camp after school, and in return for shining boots, some of the guards let me talk with a party of Texans who were laying boards over a muddy stretch of ground outside the gate.

"My brother was at Shiloh," I told them. "With the Fifty-fifth Illinois."

"Fifty-fifth?" one of the younger ones asked. "We fought 'em for a time. Drove 'em from their camps."

"No, those were Ohio boys that run," a second reb argued. "I remember those Illinoians. They were stubborn to a fault. Gave ground slowly, in good order. You'd think they was from Texas!"

"Yeah, those were the ones shot Cap'n Smith," the younger man said. "Killed some good men, too. A lot of brave fellows died on that field. For nothin'."

They paused a minute to remember. As I gazed into their wretched faces and studied the sorrow in their eyes, I imagined there was more to battle than the newspapers could guess.

"You got a name, boy?" the young rebel asked.

"Orion Howe," I told him. "I drilled here with the Fifty-fifth, but my pa won't let me join."

"Smart man, your pa," the rebel observed, clasping my hand. "My pa tried to argue me out of it, too, but I'm too mule stubborn to listen to anybody. I'm Hiram Bartlett."

"I'm Will Stephens," the older one added.

"You need anything?" I whispered.

"Everything," Bartlett answered. "Mostly food. Rations are thin in here."

"I'll bring you food if I can," I promised.

"You give the guards something, and they'll pass it through," Stephens suggested. "You got kin down South?"

"Yes," I told them. It wasn't entirely a lie, after all. Pa and L were in Tennessee, weren't they?

I spoke to Granny about taking food to the prisoners, but she wouldn't allow it.

"Orry," she objected, "it's not fitting for you to befriend those men when your father and brother are down South fighting them. I know it's your generous heart that's suggesting it, but not everyone will see it that way. It would be best to stay away from that place. There's sure to be sickness."

"I don't see how—"

"You're not to go back!" she insisted. "Besides, they're to be exchanged soon. Then they'll march back South and shoot more brave young boys."

I wanted to argue, but something in Granny's eyes hushed me.

I didn't return to Camp Douglas, but it was impossible to shut out the war. Every week some new regiment paraded down Michigan Avenue on its way to the fighting. The hospitals and hotels were full of sick and wounded soldiers. Calvin Morgan, a boy only two years older than I was, returned to school.

"They don't need one-legged soldiers," he said as he crutched his way into the classroom.

I felt like a shirker, staying behind. Lyston's letters made me feel even worse. They weren't full of adventure and good humor like the ones written before Shiloh. Instead, they told of some friend or other wounded or dying. By August the regiment was in Memphis, and every sign warned that they would soon begin the final assault that would wrest control of the Mississippi from the Confederacy.

I miss you, Orry, L wrote. I packed some spare shirts, drawers, and stockings in a flour sack and donned my old uniform. I had grown some lately, and it didn't stretch down my legs too well anymore. Still, it passed for a uniform.

"Orry?" Granny said when I appeared, drum at my side.

"I've waited long enough," I told her. "I'll be fourteen in a few months, and there's not a handful of boys that old left in my class. I ought to be with Pa and L."

"They ought to be here with you," she argued.

"One way or another," I told her. "I can get a train to the river and catch a steamer down to Memphis. The Fifty-fifth's short of drummers. You read that yourself."

"Your father didn't send for you."

"L did. I read it in his letters. Once I get down there, I can convince Pa to agree to it."

"It's hundreds of miles to Memphis," she objected. "You can't go by yourself. We'll write your father. If he agrees to your enlisting, you can go down there with some officer."

"Granny, I love you," I said, kissing her forehead. "Just the same, I'm going. Don't you see? I have to."

 FOUR

All through those last weeks of August, I had felt as if the war was passing me by. Suddenly I was determined to catch up with it. In my homemade uniform, I passed easily enough for a soldier, and no one at the Chicago and Alton depot gave me more than a second glance. It wasn't until the westbound train rolled into motion that anyone said a word to me.

"Conductor's coming," a thin-faced boy no more than a year older than me whispered as he paused beside my seat in the rear of the car. "Got a ticket?"

"I'm military," I announced nervously.

"Sure," he mumbled. "Got a pass?"

"No," I confessed.

"Then you'd do best to follow me," he advised. "Don't worry. I helped plenty of fellows run off to join the war. I'd go too if I hadn't hired myself out to the military telegraph."

"Oh?" I asked. "What makes you think I'm running away?"

"Well, you're no soldier," he said, laughing. "Not with your blouse unbuttoned and those good shoes. More likely a schoolboy. Button up and look neat when you're on a train. You ought to've cut your hair shorter, too. Well, try limping and keep your eyes down like you're bothered about something. And for Pete's sake keep clear of conductors. They've got no sympathy for boys running off to be soldiers. Not if they cheat the C and A out of fare money!"

I nodded and followed the boy obediently. We hid for a time between the second and third car. Once the conductor passed us, I breathed a sigh of relief.

"I'm Orion Howe," I told my companion in crime. "My pa and brother are with the Fifty-fifth Illinois in Memphis. I'm joining them."

"I'm Cully McCracken," he replied, shaking my hand. "Pa's been dead since Wilson's Creek, but I've got three brothers somewhere near Memphis, serving under Grant. You run across one of 'em, tell him to write."

"My brother writes sometimes," I told Cully. "The letters haven't been too cheerful since Shiloh."

"That was a mean fight, yes, sir," Cully observed. "I've met more'n a few fellows shot up last April thereabouts. I used to figure after a bit, once I got a little older, I'd join Bob, the youngest of my brothers, and we'd soldier side by side. He's just sixteen, though, and he's scared that if I signed on they might guess he was underage himself."

"My brother's a little more than a year younger than I am. So that argument won't work with me. You can see how it is. I can't be the only man in my family to stay home."

"Sure you can't," Cully agreed. "You going to beat a drum then?"

"That's right," I boasted. "Pa's the regimental fife major, and I drummed for the boys when they were learning their

34

drill. I don't imagine they'll turn me down when I get there."

"Got to get there, though," Cully pointed out. "It's a long way from Alton to Memphis. You can't swim it! Best thing to do is get aboard a steamer at Alton. Get off at Cairo, down at the tip of Illinois. You can try to find someone at the supply depot who can get you in with some teamsters hauling Grant's supplies. Don't offer anybody money, though. They've been known to cut a throat or two. If they think you're a poor orphan off to join the army, they'll likely consider it good sport to smuggle you past the officers."

"I thought I'd catch a packet at St. Louis and go straight to Memphis," I told Cully. "Wouldn't that be easier?"

"It would if anybody was sailing that far south," Cully replied. "No regular sailings beyond Cairo nowadays. You take my advice. Go with the teamsters."

I did. It wasn't easy, though. Dodging the railroad conductor was a game compared to staying clear of the steamboat men. I don't think a one of them stood less than six feet tall, and the three biggest went well past two hundred pounds. We weren't ten miles past St. Louis when they tossed two stowaways right into the Mississippi River! I hid behind crates of rifles and boxes of dry biscuit. I crawled inside an empty ammunition chest and slept there one whole night. They finally found me the morning we were due to reach Cairo.

"Knew there was a boy here," one of them snarled. "Look at this!" he cried as he lifted me by one shoulder and dangled me like a dead rat. "Little Yankee. Too small to keep. Best we throw him back!"

35

"Hold on there!" a woman suddenly shouted.

"Unhand the lad," a deeper, commanding voice ordered.

The steamboat man released me, and I fell in a heap on the deck. Before I could make my escape, a bewhiskered man wearing the single star of a brigadier general on his tailored blue uniform clamped a firm hand on my shoulder.

"Deserter?" he asked.

"No, sir," I answered. "Truth is, I'm still trying to join up."

"Thought so, Henry," the woman remarked. "Another one of your boy heroes."

"Have you got family back home?" the general asked.

"Yes, sir," I confessed, "but not so much as is in the army. I can beat the drum, sir. I know every call. I played for the recruits, both at Waukegan and in Chicago. Pa says drummers have a job to do, just the same as soldiers. Well, I can drum as good as anybody twice my age, so it seems to me that's what I ought to do."

I don't think I convinced the general of anything, but he and his wife interceded with the boat captain, and I stepped ashore at Cairo with dry feet. From there I made my way along the riverfront to the sprawling supply depot. I admit the teamsters appeared to be a tough lot, and I recalled Cully's warning. I rolled up the few dollars I possessed and stuffed them in my right shoe before approaching a tall, sweat-streaked sergeant.

"Sir, are those wagons yonder headed for General Grant?" I asked.

"Who wants to know?" he replied. "You'd be the general's aide, no doubt. No rebel spy would come in here dressed in such a poor example of an army uniform."

"I guess it would be wrong to tell me where you're going," I said, scratching my chin. With Missouri across the Mississippi River to the west and Kentucky across the Ohio River just south, Cairo was just about the last tip of free state. Even so, southern Illinois had its share of pro-Southern sympathizers. I once heard that if you threw ten Cairo men into a basket and shook it up, a reb spy was as like as not to be the first to fall out.

"Just what business would you be having with General Grant?" the sergeant demanded to know.

"None," I answered. "The Fifty-fifth Illinois is at Memphis, though, and I plan to join them there. I'll been their new drummer, you see."

"Memphis, eh? Too bad you weren't here Tuesday last. We had two transports bound for Memphis. We could've put you on either one and no one'd been the wiser. Now, well, it's a puzzle."

"Yes, sir," I agreed.

"Hey, Peterson!" the sergeant called. "You interested in some company?"

A skinny corporal poked his head around a barrel of molasses. "Him?" Peterson asked. "Not much company."

"Wouldn't be much load for the mules, either," the sergeant observed. "Headed for the Fifty-fifth, he is."

"Fine regiment," Corporal Peterson remarked. "One of the early outfits. You'd no doubt be taking the place of one of the dead ones."

"Maybe," I said, growing cold at the notion. "Might be somebody who was just sick, though."

"Sick, dead, it's all the same," the sergeant muttered. "The Mississippi River south of Cairo is all fevers and pestilence. We'd best get our men out of Memphis and finish up this war before the whole army's in a hospital."

"Don't pay him no mind, son," Corporal Peterson said, waving me to his side. "It's not half so bad as he'd have you think. Now, you want to get to Memphis, do you? I can get you close, but you might still have a day and a half's walk. You can manage that, can't you?"

"In my sleep," I boasted.

I expected the hard part to be talking myself onto a wagon. That proved simple enough. The difficulties lay ahead. First I had to help Corporal Peterson and the other teamsters load their wagons. Then I helped steady the skittish mules while a steamer ferried us across the Ohio River into Kentucky. From there we began the long trek overland across that state and into Tennessee. All the while we saw farm boys and women watching. Kentucky hadn't joined the Confederacy, and following the fighting at Shiloh the rebel army had abandoned most of Tennessee. Lately, though, the rebels under General Braxton Bragg had started north, bypassing Nashville and threatening central Kentucky.

It was hard to know whether the Kentucky and Tennessee farms we passed were loyal or secessionist. When a handful of riders appeared one afternoon, though, we had few doubts as to their intentions.

"Raiders," Corporal Peterson warned. "We'll see more of them tonight."

And so it was that I had my first taste of fighting rebels before I was even mustered into my regiment. The teamsters formed a box corral with the wagons so that the animals were secure within. Our little cavalry escort, half a company of Indianans, kept watch while we did our best to get some rest under the wagon beds. Corporal Peterson snored away like there was no tomorrow, but I was too nervous to sleep.

The raiders struck two hours after dusk. They raced in from three directions, scattered our escort, and plucked two wagons from the southern side of the box. They next drove half the mules off and did their best to panic the rest. By then another whole company of our cavalry had appeared, and the frustrated Confederates contented themselves with their two wagons. They set three others afire, but the light only helped our horse soldiers retrieve some of the stolen mules.

I passed the raid beside a wheel, praying the rebels would stay away. I wasn't much use to anybody. I had no gun. I couldn't even steady the men by beating a drum. When it was over, I helped extinguish a burning wagon. Then, when dawn lit the eastern horizon, I climbed atop Corporal Peterson's wagon and resumed my journey.

The wagon raid helped me realize how suddenly things could change in the middle of a war. One moment I had ridden securely along a road. The next I was cowering behind a wagon wheel, fearful for my very life. I supposed that of all the fears a soldier must face, it was the unknown, the unexpected, and the unpredictable that he most dreaded. I didn't doubt that I could face anything, no matter how awful, so long as I could see it and know what to expect. But after the wagon raid, I never in all my life slept as soundly at night.

One good thing came of the raid, though. Our scarcity of mules brought help. The captain of our escort telegraphed Memphis, and a small party arrived with additional animals the following day. When the wagons reached the main depot at Jackson, Tennessee, the Memphis teamsters turned for home. I went with them.

My year in Chicago had educated me in the ways of cities, and I had recently viewed St. Louis from the Mississippi River. I expected Memphis to be a similar metropolis. It wasn't. From the landward side, the place appeared little different from some of the depot towns that lined the railroad. Along the river, the city took on a somewhat grander appearance. There were some lovely homes, most of them painted white or built of red brick. Several large hotels and warehouses had been converted to hospitals or barracks.

I took a brief tour of the city before seeking out the Fifty-fifth Illinois. Down at the river I gazed enviously at a handful of black-skinned boys dipping fishing rods in the shallows. Not far away an old woman sat on her porch, scowling as a company of blue-clad troops marched past.

"Mind my flowers there, boy!" she shouted as a lanky young man in brown woolen trousers and a striped shirt raced past. She suddenly threw her cane forward, and the boy tripped and fell. I couldn't help laughing.

"Old hag," the boy complained as he rubbed a skinned knee.

"You sound like Chicago," I said, stepping over and helping him up.

"Am," he said as he regained his senses. "She shouldn't treat a federal soldier like that."

"I guess she doesn't know she's lost the war," I said. "You a soldier?"

"Close to it," he replied. "Name's Charley Quinn. I've come to enlist."

"Orion Howe," I said, shaking his hand. "Me, too."

"They'll never believe you're eighteen, Howe," he argued. "You'd be better off trying the Navy. They're short-handed, what with all the new gunboats we're building."

"I've come to join my pa and brother," I told him. "They're with the Fifty-fifth Illinois, camped here in Memphis."

"Less'n a mile from this very spot," Charley told me. "You know those boys?"

"I drummed for them when they were training. They've had losses, and I hope they'll have a place for me."

"Figure they might take me, too?" Charley asked.

"We can go and ask," I suggested. "Come on. Show me the way."

I followed Charley a quarter mile to where dozens of regimental camps spread out from the river. The Fifty-fifth was in a fine, well-drained spot, and the soldiers had improved the place by building makeshift huts to replace their tattered conical Sibley tents. The men were mostly sewing patches on torn garments, cleaning their weapons, or playing cards. I spotted Lyston and Joe Edwards scribbling letters beside the orderly tent.

"I guess you're feeling fitter, eh, L?" I called.

Lyston set his pen aside a moment and listened hard. He couldn't quite believe what he was hearing, and I had to speak a second time before he glanced around to see if it was really me. When he spied my face, he jumped to his feet and raced over. He flew the last five feet, and I caught him for a moment in my arms. Of course, even at four feet four inches, he was more than I could hold for long. He toppled me, and we lay in a heap, wrestling like brothers

41

will and stirring up dust until Colonel Malmborg marched out from his tent across the way and ordered us silent.

"Vat's de meaning of dis?" he growled.

"My brother Orion's come to visit," Lyston explained. When the colonel's left eyebrow flickered, Lyston scrambled to his feet, stiffened his spine, and saluted.

"Sorry, sir," L said, steadying himself. "We didn't mean to disturb you."

"No, sir," I agreed.

"You drummed at de camp in Chicago?" Malmborg asked.

"Yes, sir," L explained. "Better'n anybody. He could take Phil Pitts's place with Company C. Phil's a good soldier but a terrible drummer."

"It's the truth," Joe agreed. "Orry taught the rest of us the calls."

"You want to join up?" the colonel asked.

"Yes, sir," I answered. "I came down here to do just that. Of course, Pa's here to sign for me."

"Figure he'll agree?" a familiar voice asked from behind my left shoulder.

"He might," I said, turning to face him. "He'd know how determined we Howes are when we set our mind on a thing. I got down here from Chicago on my own, Pa, and I plan to stay."

"Please, Pa," Lyston pleaded. "Company C needs a drummer, and you know Orry can do the job."

"What about school?" Pa asked.

"There's hardly anyone left to teach classes," I argued. "I sit there, the oldest boy in school who still has all his arms and legs. I can't bear to watch the others stare at me, Pa.

42

They whisper to each other, but I know what they're thinking. There's Orion Howe. His little brother's serving so he can shirk."

"No one's required to join the army at your age. Not even fourteen," Pa grumbled. "You won't be eighteen for better than four more years. Your grandmother—"

"Granny Howe could fight the best division in Bob Lee's army and make 'em sorry for it," I insisted. "I belong here, Pa. There will be time for school later."

"Company C could use him, Will," Joe added. "Poor Pitts is all thumbs."

"Fife Major, vat do you tink?" Colonel Malmborg asked.

"I suppose you had better add his name to the muster, colonel," Pa said, resting his hands on my shoulders. "Wouldn't do for Company C to falter."

"No sir," Joe said, grinning at Lyston. "Wouldn't do at all."

 FIVE

Colonel Malmborg attended to the enlistment papers personally. Before you could shake a stick, Charley Quinn and I were members of the Fifty-fifth. Afterward, the quartermaster provided us with proper uniforms. Charley set off to join Company B. Lyston and Joe led me over to Company C's line of tents, where Phil Pitts in particular celebrated my arrival.

"Glad to swap this devil of a drum for my old rifle," Phil said, passing over his drum. "You're welcome to it, Howe. More'n welcome!"

Some of the other Company C soldiers were less enthusiastic.

"Not another Waukegan boy," Henry Woodring complained when I began practicing. "Aren't there any full-grown bodies left in Illinois?"

"We can't all be giants," I said, smiling at Woodring. "Some have to be small enough so the men in the back rows have a chance to shoot their rifles."

"I like Woodring up front myself," Phil declared. "He

44

makes such a fine target that the rest of us are a good deal safer."

That night I slept between Lyston and Joe Edwards in a log shelter they had crafted just behind the colonel's tent. I slept like a log, and before I knew it John Curtiss, one of our sergeants, roused me from my bed and sent me out into the cool, misty morning air to beat reveille for Company C. The other drummers were already at work, and I simply lent my drumming to the sounds drifting across the scattered camps. It was quite a sight, watching the soldiers stumble out of their beds, half dressed and unshaven. Company C was a real shambles. As Sergeant Curtiss called the roll, Colonel Malmborg gave us a sour stare.

"That won't do, Howe," Francis Shaw, the company commander, scolded after the men returned to their tents to ready themselves for breakfast. "Company C's never to be the last at attention again. Tomorrow I expect to be first."

After I beat breakfast call, Sergeant Curtiss led me over to Phil Pitts and two other private soldiers, George Crowell and the sergeant's brother, Henry.

"You bring your gear over from the drummers' tents," the sergeant commanded. "These boys will share their mess with you."

Now calling the others *boys* was a stretch. Phil was already twenty-one, and the others were past thirty! I had hoped to pass some of my soldiering time with my brother.

"Sergeant—" I started to object.

"Don't worry," Henry said, clamping his hand over my mouth. "We'll tend to him, Johnny."

I wasn't certain that I liked the sound of it. In truth, the

45

three of them became like the big brothers I never had. They helped me sew up the overlong trousers that the quartermaster supplied; and they had me up, dressed, and drumming in plenty of time every morning. I surprised them by taking our rations, mixing in a little pepper and an onion, and transforming it into something quite decent to eat.

As my first week in the army came to an end, I settled into the routine of a drummer. After reveille and breakfast call, I announced sick call. Those men who weren't sick reported for woodcutting or other assorted duties. At eight o'clock I beat the fourth call, guard mount. That was when the current guard changed places with the new batch. Afterward Colonel Malmborg made his morning inspection. We then marched to the edge of camp and began our morning drill. I announced that with the fifth call of the day. We were supposed to practice close-order drill for the rest of the morning, but we only did that half the time. We were veterans, and although the colonel expected perfection, he often rewarded us by releasing us to the camp well before noon.

My sixth call, announcing the midday meal, was always well received. The men called it roast beef, although it was mostly pork that we had to eat. Sometimes Phil and Henry would scrounge some peas, carrots, or onions from town. On such occasions, we would combine our meat ration with another mess, drop in some potatoes, and feast on a proper stew. It worked best to put the pot on to boil after breakfast. Phil would talk one of the contraband—refugee slaves— into tending it. The town was full of those miserable folks, and they would do just about anything for us. Some regiments took terrible advantage of their efforts, but I followed

Phil's example. He prided himself on seeing every favor paid for in food, supplies, or coin, and I did the same.

The day's true highlight came after dinner, when the whole regiment assembled, arms in hand, for dress parade. We musicians joined Pa in front of the men. We drummed up a storm, playing some military air or other. We marched slowly down the line before picking up the pace on the return trip. The officers then stepped four paces in front of their companies. Each made his report. Finally, when all ten companies had reported to Colonel Malmborg, the colonel issued the day's orders. Sometimes he would make a speech. If we didn't have too much drill, there would be time to waste until supper call.

The day concluded when, after beating tattoo while the sergeants held evening roll call, I closed the company's day by beating taps.

Our ordinary routine came to an end the morning of September 9. We had barely assembled when a messenger arrived on horseback from General Morgan L. Smith, our brigade commander. I was with my company, so I knew little besides the fact that a messenger had arrived. It wasn't long before Colonel Malmborg sent for the company commanders.

"Keep the men at attention," Captain Shaw ordered as he marched off toward the colonel's tent. "We may finally have a chance to chase some rebels."

We did. Within minutes officers barked orders. The men hurried about, filling canteens and packing rations. In an hour we were marching south and east toward Hernando.

"We're going railroad-wrecking, boys!" Captain Shaw

told us. "We have a bridge to burn and perhaps some irregulars to round up."

The notion of action energized the men. I was particularly excited about marching to war at last.

"Don't expect to see any rebs, Orion," Phil warned when we took our first pause. "We're throwing up enough dust to warn rebs as far south as Mississippi. We won't do any fighting this trip."

He was right to begin with. We trudged along to Hernando that hot, dusty September morning without spying anything unusual. A barking dog followed us for three miles, but otherwise it wasn't much more than drill stretched into a straight line rather than marched back and forth across a parade ground.

At Hernando, Colonel Malmborg inspected the railroad bridge. He assigned one company to rip up the rails and a second to build fires at either end. Within an hour yellow flames licked at the dry timbers, and soon the bridge was falling in blackened ashes into the river. Meanwhile we were all growing parched, so a detail went downstream to fill canteens.

I passed my own time kindling a cook fire. By that time, most of Company C had stacked arms, and all of us were hungry. A single rifle shot then echoed down the river. In a flash the men raced to grab their weapons. Captain Shaw ordered me to beat assembly, and soon the regiment formed a fierce-looking line opposite the river.

"What's become of the water party?" someone asked.

Colonel Malmborg frowned. He dispatched a handful of skirmishers to search the river. They returned with the canteens—but no soldiers.

"We saw signs of reb horses," one of the skirmishers announced.

"Send word to the escort," the colonel shouted. "Prepare for marching."

We weren't alone that day, and it was fortunate. We had some cavalry along to scout ahead and shield us from trouble. The horse soldiers splashed across the river and rode out into the countryside. They returned two hours later with our sheepish water party.

"If you're bound to be a reb prisoner, this is the best way to do it," Phil told me. "Get yourself free that same day."

The cavalry also nabbed the reb lieutenant who had surprised and captured our detail. The rebel officer had put up somewhat of a fight, and he now appeared bruised and battered. His uniform was in tatters, and only his eyes remained defiant.

"If he's the best they can throw our way, the rebs're finished," Phil remarked.

"Don't judge a man's fight by his clothes," Henry warned. "Those Shiloh rebs weren't much to look at, either, but they killed their full share of us."

We fought no more rebels that day.

Toward the end of October rumors of a new advance southward flew through the Union camps. I thought it was about time. There we were, sitting in Memphis, guarding stores and securing the western part of Tennessee for the Union. That didn't take a regiment, much less an army. We had far too much time on our hands, and no one was more anxious than I was to get on with the war.

On October 22 the entire regiment formed in front of our camp with field packs and three days' provisions. We had high hopes of striking a new blow against the tottering Confederacy, but Colonel Malmborg explained that we were only headed out on another raid. He was answered by a momentary groan.

"Ve must do our duty as General Sherman decides it," the colonel growled. I suspected he didn't like sitting around in Memphis any better than the rest of us.

We set off in good order, marching out of town toward Shelby Depot the same way we had a dozen times before. A squadron of cavalry protected our flanks and scouted ahead. Soon, though, our careful formation dissolved into a stumbling crowd of frustrated veterans. The colonel being forward, we saw no reason to stay in rigid rank and file. What really irked us was the notion that we were devoting most of our time to preserving order in a rebel town and protecting the property of our enemy!

That changed shortly. As we marched into the depot, Colonel Stuart, our original commander, addressed us.

"Boys, we all know this place is a nest of rebels," he told us. "It seems only right that these dwellings be consumed by the fires of retribution."

It required no genius to understand the meaning of Colonel Stuart's order. Men scurried about, collecting brush. We made piles beside the doors and windows while others inspected the stores and houses for anything useful to the Union cause. Where before we were chastised for plundering, we now raided everything in sight. Not a single chicken or slice of pie escaped.

At one of the stores, some fellows from Company I were helping themselves to all kinds of goods. The helpless townspeople and shopkeepers raised howls of protest, and

Colonel Stuart finally acted. Spurring his horse, the colonel galloped over and called to the raiders. Their leader, Sergeant Fisher, attempted to escape by jumping out a window. He took a hard fall, but that was only the beginning. A private followed and landed square atop the sergeant!

You never heard such an uproar. For weeks thereafter soldiers were needling Fisher about his escapade. In truth, the burning of Shelby Depot allowed us all to let off steam. We were a calmer, happier regiment afterward.

That night we gathered around cook fires and sang. A half dozen contrabands joined us. One old man brought a fiddle, and we had a fine time. Shortly before midnight, though, a shotgun blast sent us rushing around, fetching weapons or, in my case, my drum. As I beat assembly, another blast erupted. This time one of the contrabands screamed in pain. Joe Edwards held a bandage to the poor man's bloody shoulder. Captain Joe Black and a sergeant lay facedown near the fire, but their wounds were more embarrassing than dangerous.

All our drill and rifle practice paid off because we quickly took position and swept the woods with volleys of deadly rifle fire. Nothing could have survived our onslaught. That next morning, we found nary a trace of the bushwhackers, though. They got safely away.

We were a regiment freed from the constraints of reason, and when the contrabands reported a rebel bushwhacker named Burrows responsible for the attack, we vowed vengeance. We marched to his nearby home, a lovely mansion near the crossroads town of Raleigh. His wife and grown daughters were present, but the bushwhacker and his cohorts were off skulking in the shadows. Companies E and I lit torches and prepared to burn the house, but Mrs. Burrows managed to attract some sympathy as soldiers escorted her to safety. The men moved the furniture and several trunks of clothing outside before setting the place ablaze.

In the midst of the conflagration, Mrs. Burrows began weeping. Her daughters ranted and raved, calling us all sorts of names.

"Filthy, uneducated baboons!" they yelled.

A big German from Company I, George Blahs, ambled over to her piano and began playing Bach. For a lover of music like myself, the wonderful melodies were like a tonic. The rebels listened in stunned silence. When Blahs finished, he turned to face the rebels. Both daughters gasped. A rebel musket ball had torn a gash across his face from mouth to ear, and the scar was as nasty as any I ever saw.

The house was still burning when we formed into companies and resumed our march. To the dismay of the rebels, many fine pieces of furniture and most of the bushwhacking captain's clothes left with us.

"You have no right!" Mrs. Burrows protested. "My husband's best coat! His boots!"

"He won't need 'em much longer, ma'am," Sergeant Curtiss boasted. "Once we catch up with him, he'll be past earthly cares."

I was pretty angry at the time, and I spared little sympathy for bushwhackers' families. Later, though, as I gazed at the assorted loot our men brought back to Memphis, I felt a pang or two of conscience.

"Must be a hard thing," Lyston said when we sat by the evening fire, roasting purloined ears of corn.

"What?" I asked.

"Finding yourself in the middle of the war like those girls today. I'm glad the rebels won't get near Waukegan."

"Me, too," I agreed.

It was only a couple of days later that the two of us found ourselves walking through the streets of Memphis, armed with seven greenbacks and determined to buy some carrots and potatoes. Over on Elm Street we came upon a scruffy batch of boys close to our own age.

"What you want here, little Yanks?" the tallest of them asked.

"We've come looking for vegetables," I said. I had the money well hidden in my shoe, so I never brought up the fact that we intended to pay cash for them.

"You boys've near stripped the city," a smaller boy complained. "Look here. I haven't even got shoes to wear! My sisters cry half the night for want of something to eat. Now you walk out here intending to take more."

"We didn't start the war," L pointed out.

"No?" the third one asked. "Who invited you boys down here anyhow? Not my pa, who's lying dead in Mississippi. Not my uncle, who's lost a leg. I got two brothers with Bragg, up in Kentucky, and neither is likely to get back home soon. We own no slaves, and since September we haven't even had a house. So you tell me. Is this any kind of a war to wage, starving poor people who only want to be left alone?"

I started to bark an answer, but Lyston nudged me silent.

"We've got to find a market hereabouts," he announced. "You wouldn't know where we could buy some potatoes, would you?"

53

"For cash money?" the tallest one asked.

I nervously backed away, but the young rebels seemed to lose their rage.

"My aunt keeps a garden," the littlest reb explained. "I could fetch you some potatoes, maybe carrots, too. How much you need?"

"L?" I asked, concerned.

"We need seven dollars' worth," he told the rebs. "We're the Fifty-fifth Illinois. Our camp's—"

"We'll find it," the oldest one said. "Give over the money. I'll see to the rest."

"Orry?" Lyston asked.

Reluctantly I peeled off my shoe and handed the rebs our money. The rebs eyed the greenbacks with a mixture of wonder and suspicion.

"Don't you worry over it, Yank," the tall reb assured me as he accepted the notes. "We may not like you, but we'll trade with you. I'm called Pulaski Tom, after my hometown. If we don't get your vegetables to you, it'll be because we're floating in the river."

"Wasn't worried," L replied.

"Your friend there was," Tom remarked. "Got his reasons, I suppose. You can trust me to make good on a promise, though, and you've got one from me this very minute."

Lyston and I shook hands with Tom and then with the other rebels. After they left, L sighed.

"You figure we'll ever see 'em again?" I asked.

"Sure," he told me. "Potatoes and carrots, too. Truth is, we'll fare better than if we deal with those traders at the waterfront. Generals plan their campaigns, and soldiers

54

fight them. Boys like you and me, those fellows, work things out the best we can."

L proved right about Pulaski Tom, and we had enough carrots and potatoes for three stews. We ended up doing a fair amount of business with those young rebs. It was almost possible to forget we were at war. Almost, but not entirely.

 SIX

Every Sunday during our days in Memphis, all of the regiments that were encamped there formed up for a grand review. Most of the time General William T. Sherman, our corps commander, inspected the men. Sometimes he or one of the other army generals spoke to the troops. At first it was inspiring, seeing our commanders riding their horses, cheering us with news of victories in Kentucky and Maryland. That fall, after all, was a good season for the Union cause. The rebels in Virginia had been thrown back in disarray after their brief invasion, and Braxton Bragg's Confederate army had met its match at Perryville, up in Kentucky. By November we were eager to do our part, and we were tired of what we considered profitless campaigning.

"When are we going after the reb army, general?" someone finally asked as Sherman watched us parade.

We all thought Colonel Malmborg was going to have a fit, and we halfway expected generals to rush down and search for the impudent fool. Sherman only laughed.

"Soon, boys!" he shouted.

It was the end of November before we had orders to march, though.

There were signs of the coming move before that. The quartermasters took our old, worn, ragged, smoke-stained Sibley tents off in two wagons. We rarely used our conical canvas homes, favoring makeshift shelters of assorted shapes and styles. The tents were cumbersome to transport, too. To replace them, the quartermasters issued sheets of canvas that could be buttoned together to make small tents. Each man then carried half a tent. These new shelters quickly took on the name dog tents because they were only big enough for a large dog. They were easily rolled, though, for carrying on a soldier's back.

Regiments, freed of their Sibley tents, dispensed with several heavy baggage wagons. We soldiers, though, grumbled about the need to carry additional weight, as we often walked as much as ten miles in a single day. The shelter halves displaced extra blankets and other gear. Veteran soldiers discarded their cook kits in favor of empty oyster or fruit tins.

As a result, the Fifty-fifth became famous for "flying light"—traveling with a minimum amount of baggage and able to move long distances without tying ourselves to a supply base. After receiving three days' rations on the morning of November 26, we were able to leave Memphis and march all the way to Germantown in a single day. We covered twenty-five additional miles the following two days, and by December 1, we had penetrated the Confederacy as far as the Tallahatchie River, 122 miles' marching in a week's time.

It soon became clear, though, that we were not the main

thrust of the army. General U. S. Grant and the main body remained well east of us. Often we heard the thunderous roar of artillery off in the distance. Sometimes we came upon stragglers from Confederate units driven from their lines farther north. The supplies having long since vanished in our stomachs, we scoured the country for hogs, cattle, cornmeal, honey, or anything else we might locate to appease our hunger.

The great advance came to nothing. Rebel cavalry struck Grant's supply base at Holly Springs, Mississippi, burning supplies and wrecking the railroad. The news hit us particularly hard because we had worked our way south with so much effort. We started back to Memphis December 10. Three days later we marched into town to find our comfortable old camp occupied by newcomers. Grumbling, we made a bivouac in a swampy stretch of ground near the river.

It was a disheartening time for the regiment. President Lincoln approved Colonel Stuart's promotion to brigadier general. Many of the officers, led by our chaplain, Captain Milt Haney, complained that Stuart sympathized with the enemy. All too often he had protected wealthy rebs from their proper retribution. Moreover, Stuart promised more than one officer the same promotion. That bred discontent and petty rivalry.

Being a drummer and a newcomer, I tried to avoid the heated discussions that dominated campfire chat. I was more concerned with the effort it took to keep dry in our new campsite. The first night there I paired my shelter half with Phil Pitts, but between his big feet and his snoring, I got little rest. When Chaplain Haney suggested that I tent with Lyston until we broke camp again, I hesitated, though.

"Sergeant Curtiss ordered me to stay with the company," I told him.

"Well, the whole regiment's mixed together here," the chaplain observed. "You find your brother and get some rest. We'll sort out the sergeant's wishes later."

Our new camp never really got organized. Colonel Malmborg pleaded with the captains to line up our new tents and arrange themselves, but it wasn't feasible. The weather turned cold, the ground got soggier, and no one wanted to pull up poles and move tents or people. On Saturday, December 19, rumors of another move south filled the town, and the following day the Fifty-fifth Illinois boarded the steamer *Westmoreland*. We were, at long last, resuming the campaign to wrest the Mississippi from Confederate control.

I felt different the moment I stepped on board. An odd quiet seemed to fall like a cloak across the ship. Some of the veterans studied the steamboat while others began writing notes to wives or mothers. I drifted off with Lyston and Joe Edwards to the stern so that we could study the line of transports behind us. This was no raid we were launching.

"No," Joe told me. "There's going to be a real battle this time."

"Looks like it," I admitted. "What's it like, Joe?" I asked.

He stared at his toes, and Lyston took me aside.

"It's not something you can describe," my little brother said with eyes that suddenly seemed a hundred times older. "Best thing to do is wait and see it for yourself."

"But I ought to do something to get ready for it," I argued.

"That's what I thought, too," L told me, "but there isn't anything. Until you're in a real fight, listening to those howling rebs, you can't imagine the terror of it. We're a good regiment, Orry. The men will stand and hold their ground. We drummers will be safe enough."

I didn't entirely believe him. When I talked with Phil Pitts and the Curtiss brothers, they avoided the subject.

"Don't worry, Howe," Johnny urged. "Nuisance that you are, we've grown accustomed to you. We won't let any rebels shoot you."

The only one aboard the *Westmoreland* who really understood was Charley Quinn. Charley was also new at fighting.

"It's an awful awakening, they say," Charley explained, pointing to the veterans drifting around in twos and threes. "Seeing the elephant, it's called. If you haven't seen it, no matter how many books you read, you'll never know."

I guess it's natural for a boy to turn to his pa in times of uncertainty, so I sought out Will Howe. He was forward, writing a letter to Cordelia. When he spied me, he waved me over.

"Son, it's fine to see you this morning," he announced. "I was just now thinking how you and Lyston might want to send a note along to your mother."

"She's not—"

"It wouldn't hurt you to write," Pa said, calmer than usual. "Maybe pen something for your granny, too."

"I'll tell L."

"First sit a minute," he said, leading me to a stack of crates. We each sat atop one.

"Orion, you're the elder," he reminded me. "I never thought you'd be passing your childhood in the army, but here we are. I've not been as well the past few weeks as I would have liked, and my duties have kept me away from you boys. It's always possible that something more dramatic might take me off."

"Yes, sir," I noted.

"Your brother's smaller. He's campaigned longer than you have, but he's still a small boy, truth be told. Should something unforeseen occur, he'll need your steadying hand. Your mo—Cordelia will need your help, too. Promise you'll do your best?"

"I always do, Pa," I assured him. "Nothing's going to happen to you, though."

"Of course not," he agreed, mussing my hair. "Just the same, I'll leave letters with Captain Haney. The chaplain will know what needs to be done."

I nodded. After I located Lyston, we scribbled the requested notes. Then we walked up forward and gazed out at the landscape as the steamer started downstream.

We stayed aboard the *Westmoreland* the rest of that day. On Monday we passed the city of Helena, on the Arkansas bluffs, and disembarked briefly at Friar's Point. Colonel Malmborg put us through a few hours of serious drill, and I wondered if we might be readying ourselves for an invasion of Arkansas. We marched back aboard ship that afternoon, though.

We continued to make our way down the twisting,

turning Mississippi River those next few days. On Christmas we passed Milliken's Bend. The steamers pulled up there, and we soldiers studied the far shore. Atop those treacherous bluffs stood Vicksburg, a rebel stronghold with powerful cannons that kept our ships from traveling the river. Everyone knew it was our objective. We also knew that Jefferson Davis, the rebel president, had his very own plantation nearby. Davis called the place the key to the river, and he provided a whole army for its protection.

"It's no easy task we've set ourselves, Orry," L said, settling in beside me.

"No," I agreed.

One of the sailors, a youngish sort with light blond hair that fell across his face and tickled his sky blue eyes, offered his field glasses.

"Take a closer look," he suggested. "One shot from those guns yonder will blow us and your whole regiment to perdition!"

"Oh, the Navy can deal with them," L boasted. "We're not attacking from the water. No, we'll go around and hit them from behind."

"Don't you suspect they know where you're at?" the sailor asked. "You think you can land thirty thousand men without anybody seeing you do it?"

I sighed. It seemed improbable.

"Before we're through with Vicksburg," he added, "we'll be burying a lot of you boys up there. And some of us will be sleeping in this river for all eternity."

Later that night I stood alone near the *Westmoreland*'s bow. I'd never in all my life been as lonely as I felt that moment. It wasn't the best way to spend Christmas, staring into the murky waters of the Mississippi. What are you doing here, Orion Howe? I asked myself. You've got to be crazy, joining an army and going to war!

An icy wind blew off the river and ate through the blue wool of my tunic. Not even two flannel shirts kept its bite from my ribs. I shivered. After the warm, sticky, mosquito-plagued autumn in Memphis, I expected winter would be welcome. It wasn't. The air had turned cold, and with it, my courage began to evaporate.

"Dark, isn't it?" a voice called.

"Sure is," I replied. My eyes tried to identify the speaker, but the deck lamps were covered to conceal our passage. Mist shrouded his face.

"Thinking of home?" he asked as he came closer. I saw it was Rienzi Cleveland, one of my fellow Company C soldiers. He was just nineteen himself. He gazed out over the rail, looking northward.

"Not really much home to think about," I told him.

"Sure," he said. "You've got your brother here and your father, too."

"We Howes are well represented in the ranks," I said, borrowing one of Pa's favorite phrases. "Of course, drumming isn't like carrying a rifle, standing in the front line."

"There's no place to hide on a battlefield, Orry. If there was, I'd know about it. I tried to find one when the rebs charged us at Shiloh, but the truth is, there just isn't. I saw a fellow, full colonel I think he was, sitting in his tent with breakfast spread out on a table in front of him. Only trouble was that a cannon ball had flown by and carried off his head."

I shuddered. We'd lost a quarter of the regiment at

Shiloh, and there were rumors flying that we were coming up against some of those same rebs. One out of four of us might be lying on the ground, bleeding or dying or dead, before another night passed. It sounded bad enough, but even worse when you realized the ones dying would be your friends or even your brother!

I rubbed my hands together, and he rested a hand on my shoulder.

"You'll do fine," he assured me. "Scared as we were at Shiloh, we stood and fought. You're with a good bunch, you know."

"I know," I said. "I'm just afraid I'll—"

"Run?" he asked. "Not you, Orry. You'll be too busy banging away on that drum. That's the best thing to do, concentrate on your job."

"And when the shooting starts?"

"Trust us to keep you safe. You'll probably be back with the surgeon. And after all, you're a small target."

I smiled. Rienzi was no giant himself.

He left then, and I went back to staring at the river. The moon overhead illuminated the bow wave, and I imagined for a moment that it was snow. If I had stayed in Chicago the way Pa wanted, I might be sledding down a hill or enjoying a cup of hot cider with my friends following an evening of caroling.

"Brrr," a softer, high-pitched voice whimpered.

"Lyston?" I gasped. "It's too cold for you to be out here. You'll take sick again."

"If it's too cold for me, it's too cold for you," he replied, grabbing my hand and tugging on it. "Let's go below."

"Later," I said, shaking free of his hand.

"Now," he insisted. "You ought to rest. You won't get much tomorrow."

"Probably not," I said. Reluctantly, I allowed him to drag me toward the hatch. We stumbled down the rough wooden steps together. Most boys closing in on their fourteenth birthday wouldn't let a younger, littler boy boss them around, but then Lyston was my brother. He was only a year and a half younger, and so far as soldiering was concerned, *he* was the veteran.

"Worried?" he asked when we sat down together at the base of the steps.

"Some," I admitted. "What's it going to be like?"

"Not so bad as Shiloh. They came at us out of nowhere that day. I'd just finished making up a cooking fire, and I hadn't had time to get properly dressed. I never got my tunic on, so I had to fight all day in my shirt. Tore my britches to pieces on briers! Once it was over, I took fever and close to died!"

"I did die," Joe Edwards said, joining us.

"What?" I asked, staring hard at him.

"I was dead, or so most thought," Joe added with a wink of his eye. "The regiment was shot up awfully at Shiloh, a quarter of us bleeding or dead, and I was helping out the surgeons. Half the night I was up, fetching water or bathing feverish heads. Finally I just stumbled off and fell asleep."

"He lay down outside the surgeon's tent," Lyston said.

"I'm telling this story!" Joe objected. "Well, you being new to the army, don't know that when a man dies, they carry him outside and lay him ready for burying. So, there I'm sleeping, dead to the world and covered with blood from all the wounded I've been treating. The men start laying the dead alongside. One or two, then ten or twenty. I wake up surrounded! They're to the right and left, fore and aft, and I think maybe the rebs got me in my sleep. Just then a couple of fellows start loading the corpses in a wagon. I feel a tug on my leg, and I jump up, screaming."

" 'Don't go using me for a header,' he yelled!" Lyston recounted. "I don't know who was spooked more, Joe or the men who saw his corpse come to life!"

I found myself laughing along with them, and for a moment, my fear left me.

"Were you scared much?" I asked Lyston after Joe left.

"Some," he said, frowning. "Especially when men all around me started falling. The colonel steadied us up, though. Mostly we were mad about fighting on a Sunday and losing our camps. Rebs ate our breakfast, you know."

"You never did like anybody borrowing your things," I noted. "And you can't spare food."

"You're almost as skinny," he claimed, tapping my ribs. "Well, maybe not."

I grabbed him and wrestled him to the floor. We tangled ourselves and squawked considerably until a couple of sergeants from Company B separated us. That being Lyston's company, they naturally took his side and gave me an undeserved whack on the rump.

"Get some rest, children," Captain Shaw shouted from down the passageway.

"He talking to you?" I asked the sergeants.

"Couldn't be talking to you lads," the taller of the two answered. "Fine, tall, hairy-chinned pair you are, letting your young mates draw a captain's eye."

I grinned, and they helped us to our feet.

"They'll be no more of it now, will there?" the second sergeant asked.

"No, sir," I promised.

"At least not tonight," Lyston added.

After they left, Lyston led me along to the crowded hold, where our half of the regiment was quartered.

"Do you ever wonder what we're doing here?" I asked Lyston as we spread our blankets on the cold, moist deck.

"No," he answered. "I feel like I belong here."

"I try to feel that way, but mostly I feel out of step. The others are taller and older, and they know what's going to happen. Me—"

"Truth is, Orry, nobody knows what's going to happen. Not even Colonel Malmborg, though he'll never admit it. Look at the marches we've been on. We don't know whether we'll find a smokehouse to liberate or rebel cavalry to fight. Nobody really does. But whatever it is, you'll face it better with some rest."

I started to argue, but L had this sort of know-it-all look on his face. For a boy not four and a half feet tall, he could appear almost wise at times. I sighed, rolled over on my side, and tried to sleep. Mostly, though, I just lay there, wondering about tomorrow.

 SEVEN

The next morning we left the wide, rolling Mississippi for the muddier, narrow waters of the Yazoo River. The *Westmoreland* churned along with its sister transports more than ten miles before tying up at the Johnston Plantation. Nearby, the other transports carrying General Morgan Smith's brigade made their landings. Soon the various regiments were stumbling down gangways, glad to be back on solid ground.

"Are we going to drill some more?" I asked Sergeant Curtiss when he ordered me to beat assembly.

"Not this time," he answered. "This time's for real, lad. You do just what I tell you to, hear? And when the fighting commences, fall back with the other musicians. Your pa will be there to help get you organized."

"Organized for what?" I asked.

"To help with the wounded," Sergeant Curtiss explained. "You won't do us a lot of good along the skirmish line, but a drummer can carry a stretcher as well as anyone."

I swallowed hard. Looking around at the faces of the men filled me with dread. I didn't know all of their names, but every single one of them had offered a smile, a cheerful bit of advice, or even a prankish kick in the trousers. They were more than friends. And a little farther on, beating assembly for Company B, was Lyston. Pa was sure to be nearby, too. By then we all knew we were attacking no bridge or bushwhacker camp.

"Ve are striking at Vicksburg," Colonel Malmborg told us. "Ve are de sword of justice!"

"Union forever!" Company I shouted as one. All of us echoed the sentiment.

As soon as General Steele's division untangled its regiments from the boggy ground and started inland, we began our own march. In all there were thirty thousand of us in what some general had dubbed the Fifteenth Army Corps. We simply thought of ourselves as Billy Sherman's boys. Ahead of us lay Vicksburg, the choicest prize in the Confederacy save perhaps Richmond.

We trudged through seas of cockleburs and slogged through swamp all that day and part of the next. It was mostly uneventful marching. A Company D private, despite orders to the contrary, marched with a loaded rifle. He stumbled on a dislodged root, the rifle discharged, and he lost himself a considerable portion of his nose.

"Little Chris," one of his comrades said, "you've gone and spoilt your good looks."

"Didn't have much to begin with," a Company E man added. "Nor sense, either."

The men might have spared some sympathy for their unhappy friend had not every one of them considered how it might have been they themselves shot by such a careless man!

Not long afterward Colonel Malmborg rode past us.

69

"Keep at it, men," he urged. "Ve're closing on the rebels."

We quickened our pace. The notion that we were the ones surprising the graycoats this time had considerable appeal. Any hope of striking a sudden blow vanished as we picked up signs of reb scouts here and there. Twice men fired at us from ambush, but we saw no one else.

What miserable country for a fight, I thought as we continued marching. It was difficult to see anything, much less an enemy, more than ten feet away. We did come across a meeting of the generals, though. Our old colonel, David Stuart, stood with his new stars gleaming in the light of a small campfire. Sherman, Morgan Smith, Steele, and two others conferred about the best way to tackle the rebs. Meanwhile the Fifty-fifth passed two other regiments and established itself as the vanguard of the division.

"How about that?" Sergeant Curtiss asked. "The place of honor."

"What?" I asked.

"Some deem it an honor to lead the attack," Henry explained.

"Me, I'd just as soon bring up the rear," Phil grumbled.

"Now, Howe, back to the rear," the sergeant said, turning me around. It wasn't long before the other drummers likewise appeared behind the line of uniformed soldiers.

"Give us a tune," someone called.

"Boys," Pa said, "it's time to show off your training. 'Battle Cry of Freedom.' "

I never, not in all my life, heard a song create such a stir. As I beat my drum and sang, others up and down the line took up the refrain.

"Oh we'll rally 'round the flag, boys,
we'll rally 'round the flag,
Singing the Battle Cry of Freedom!"

It was more than simply stirring. We marched into battle like a wave of crusaders. The bayonets glinted in the sunlight, and my heart was full and warm with determination.

"That's enough," Pa declared as the men reached the swampy expanse known as Chickasaw Bayou. Just south of us lay the Chickasaw Bluff, and beyond that was Vicksburg, sleepily dozing while the wolves were baying at the back door.

"See anything?" L asked as I stared through the mist at the slope beyond the bayou.

"No," I replied. "The rebs are up there, though."

"How do you know?" Joe Edwards objected.

Suddenly the singing stopped. A sheet of flame illuminated the crest of the bluff for just an instant. Men fell, and our line wavered. A battery of six-pounders opened up behind us, and officers tried to form their units in two lines. The men hesitated, and when a fresh volley exploded from the bluff, our lines began to unravel.

"Ignore 'em, boys!" General Smith shouted as he rode along our line, plumed hat in hand.

"They've got some good shots up that hill, general!" Henry Curtiss warned.

"No, they can't—"

At that very moment the general halfway hopped out of his saddle. He eased back down, but any fool could see he had been shot. He was bleeding severely from the hip. He appeared reluctant to leave the battlefield, though.

When the general decided he had no choice but to retire to his tent, Colonel Malmborg made a similar ride to raise our spirits. You had to say this for the little Swede: He did know how to make an impression.

The colonel soon departed, but he returned with batteries A and B of the Illinois Artillery. Their long-barreled twenty-pounder Parrot guns moved forward, supported by the lead companies of our regiment. The artillery duel raged for several minutes. No one had a real advantage, and it accomplished little other than blowing boulders and rock splinters out of the bluff. Rifle fire aimed our way proved deadlier. Dozens of men fell every few minutes.

The noise was deafening, and the air filled with a mixture of odors. Gunpowder mixed with sweat. I sniffed something new, too. Death. It was oddly sweet at first, like a smoke-house in February. Gradually it soured until I felt that I would choke from it. Powder and suffering tainted the air with an acid, sulfurous taste.

"L?" I asked, looking with wild eyes at my brother.

"Just keep down," he advised. "Less likely to hit what they can't see."

Pa said pretty much the same thing, but when Joe Edwards leaped up and raced over to help a wounded Company I man, I crept forward.

Our regiment was trapped at the base of the bluff, with rebels firing on us from two sides. Occasionally a man would claw his way up the steep embankment, but each time one got close to the crest, he was shot down. That's what happened to Charley Quinn.

I guess maybe you can be so scared of being a coward

that you throw away every ounce of good sense. Charley shed his pack, slid his bayonet into place, and raced toward the bluff. He was agile, and it seemed as if he might elude the rebel bullets. Then he threw up his hands and fell.

I rushed through the ranks of shaken men to where he lay. "Charley?" I whispered. "Charley?"

Blood trickled from a single red hole in his forehead. He didn't move. I grabbed his legs and hauled him back to the rear. Later, when I looked in his pocket, I found three letters. One was for his folks. The second was for a girl. Charley liked to talk about one. The final one bore Colonel Malmborg's name. It requested he be taken home. The first letters were mailed, but Charley's request was ignored. He was buried with the other dead in that infernal rebel swamp.

We weren't the only ones caught in the maelstrom of death. The Fifty-fourth Ohio, our brothers since the whirlwind of Shiloh, marched up in support. They were soon staggered by three accurate volleys. The Thirteenth Illinois lost its colonel. The Sixth Missouri managed to cross a sandbar and got a few men close to one of the rebel parapets. Rebel reinforcements drove the Missourians back into the swamp.

In the end the Fifty-fifth got off lightly. We lost eight men. The Fifty-fourth Ohio lost nineteen soldiers. The Sixth Missouri had fourteen dead and forty-three wounded. As for the Thirteenth Illinois, they were shot to pieces. Twenty-seven of their best men lost their lives trying to take the rebel position. One hundred and seven more suffered wounds. Thirty-nine became prisoners.

The army as a whole got nowhere in its attempt to slip through Vicksburg's back door.

"Rebs bolted it shut," Sergeant Curtiss observed. "We may have ourselves another try at it, though."

I think General Sherman planned to do just that, but Providence intervened. That night a tremendous storm lashed at us. Wet, cold, and exhausted, we began collapsing in heaps. Eventually the colonels withdrew their regiments a quarter mile onto better ground. That was fortunate because the river swept up over its levees and flooded Chickasaw Bayou beyond recognition.

I sat beside a small fire that night, trembling from cold more than fear and remembering Charley Quinn.

"I didn't see any elephant," I told Lyston, "but I got a taste of war. It's not what I thought at all."

"I know," L replied.

"I wasn't half as scared as I thought I'd be."

"So it wasn't so bad as you figured, Orry?"

"Maybe not that part of it," I noted. "There was something else, though."

"What?"

"I didn't think about how I'd feel when a friend died. L, you won't go making any fool charges, will you?"

"I was at Shiloh, remember?" he said, leaning against me. "I've seen plenty of dead men, and I can't say I favor the way they look."

"No, and I wouldn't want my brother numbered among them."

"You were pretty foolish yourself, Orry," he added. "Don't you go and get dead, either. I expect to require your help with my schooling when this is over."

"No, you're as smart as anyone I know. You may need me to introduce you to a girl or two, though."

"Since when?" he asked, grinning. "I'm not the one who never gets kissed."

We commenced a fine argument then. When it was over, Lyston peered up at the rain and sighed.

"I was hoping for better weather," he said. "I know you like to count the stars on your birthday."

"Huh?"

"It's December twenty-ninth, Orry," Lyston said, shaking his head. "You're fourteen today."

I'd totally forgotten. Things being in the state they were, we had little chance of celebrating.

We remained in the swamp opposite Chickasaw Bluff until the new year dawned. We learned on New Year's Day that Bragg had fought a second bloody battle in southern Tennessee, stunning General William Rosecrans but failing to drive him from the field. In fact, when all was said and done, Bragg was the one who retreated. In Virginia we fared far worse. Our boys were butchered by the thousands north of Richmond trying to scale a fortified ridge.

"It's time our generals learned that you can't throw your men away in pointless charges," I heard Captain Shaw complain. "Nor can you let them suffer and die in godforsaken swamps."

Maybe some generals did learn. On January 2 Sherman decided that losing a couple of thousand soldiers in a failed try to breach the rebel defenses was enough of a mistake. We marched aboard our transports and started back down the Yazoo to the Mississippi River.

"We don't look like much of an army these days,"

Captain Shaw chastised us. "Let's step lively and get our gear sorted."

No matter how neat and trim we managed to get ourselves, we couldn't ignore the fact that as a regiment, we were shrinking daily. At January muster the Fifty-fifth Illinois Volunteer Infantry Regiment boasted only 409 soldiers, and the war seemed no nearer its conclusion than the year before.

 EIGHT

Although we were defeated in our assault on the rebels at Chickasaw Bluffs, we remained convinced that we would triumph in the end. Even if we had to return to Memphis a dozen times, defeated, we were certain that we would get into Vicksburg eventually. Not everyone was so sure. The War Department questioned General Sherman's capabilities, and they replaced him as our army commander with John McClernand, a former Illinois congressman.

"If I wanted a speech, I'd go right to McClernand," Pa remarked. "Billy Sherman's the man to lead an army."

We Illinoians were upset about something else. A couple of newspapers from southern Illinois circulated through the fleet, and their Southern sympathies outraged us.

"Nothing but snakes!" Phil declared.

"Sure," Henry agreed. "Copperheads. That's what they're called."

The newspapers urged the population to defy the draft. It suggested soldiers desert their regiments. Lincoln was a tyrant! Grant was a criminal!

"They're as bad as the rebels," Captain Shaw grumbled as he cast one of the papers into the river.

"Worse," Sergeant Curtiss insisted. "The rebels make no pretense as to their true colors."

We soon drew up petitions requesting permission to march north and punish the traitorous newspaper editors.

"This is crazy, boys," Captain Shaw said when we asked him to sign. "We're a far sight more useful here than we would be up north!"

Of course, we all knew no one was going to let us leave the army, but our petition did lift everyone's spirits. It wasn't as good as a victory, but it was a far sight better than another defeat.

As it turned out, General McClernand did not intend to take us back to Memphis. Instead, we left the Mississippi River and steamed west up the Arkansas. Our destination was Fort Hindman, at what was called the Post of Arkansas, or Arkansas Post. A rebel garrison of five thousand men there protected the water approach to Little Rock, the state capital. In the past, raiding parties had come down from Fort Hindman to attack our supply boats. McClernand thought our army, almost thirty thousand strong, could easily capture the rebel garrison and eliminate the threat.

No matter how you figured it, the coming battle offered us a fine chance for victory. We outnumbered the enemy six to one, and we had a whole fleet of gunboats along to provide supporting fire from the river. The rebels could escape by retreating and blowing up their fort, but nobody expected them to do that.

Our fleet dropped anchor January 9, and regiments began

going ashore the following day. The Fifty-fifth Illinois landed around noon at Notrib's Farm, three miles below the fort. There was just a narrow strip of good, solid land separating the river from the swampy ground beyond. We were only one of the regiments crowding together there.

"Howe, beat that drum of yours," Sergeant Curtiss shouted. "Company C, form up."

I took out my sticks and began drumming. I didn't see what use it was, what with dozens of drummers doing the same thing and no drum all that different from the next. I had been in the army long enough to know it was best to do what the sergeant said, though. Soon the company linked up with the regiment, and before long, we set off toward the rebel works.

After marching almost a mile, we encountered a line of rebels manning rifle pits. Other rebels raised dust as they hurried back toward their fort. We formed a line and began advancing slowly.

"Get back, son," Captain Shaw scolded me. "Here," he added, tying a white kerchief across my arm. "Now they can see you're a noncombatant."

I wanted to continue on with the men, but Pa's heavy hand held me back.

"We have a job to do," he reminded me.

"He's right," Chaplain Haney added, motioning for us to lie down. "We have to tend the wounded. You're as important as any man carrying a gun. More so to a soldier who's bleeding. You can save his life, boys. Be alert for a chance."

All I could think about was Charley Quinn, who had joined the regiment with me and was now dead.

"I see someone told you about the cloth this time," Joe Edwards said as he settled in beside me. "I don't know that it helps, but we do it anyway."

"Makes a better target for the rebel sharpshooters," Lyston said, smiling.

"I don't know that we have much to fear from them," I said, pointing at the rebels fleeing up the road with our skirmishers in rapid pursuit.

As we got closer, we had our first glimpse at Fort Hindman. It was maybe three hundred feet in length down any of its four squared sides. Powerful cannons frowned out of four massive bastions. The walls appeared to be fifteen feet thick, and the ground all around was well protected by rifle pits.

"We'll never get near the place," Lyston said, shaking his head. "They can blast us from up there with their big guns while we're hopelessly out of range."

I wasn't worried, though. Our gunboats had already opened up a sharp fire on the fort. The army's artillery batteries pushed their cannons ever closer, and soon the powerful voices of the twenty-pounders joined the onslaught.

Along with the Fifty-fourth and Fifty-seventh Ohio, we advanced through thick woods, cutting a road for the artillery to follow. The rebels appeared now and then, but whenever we fired on them, they broke and ran. It wasn't until we got to within rifle range of the fort itself that we halted.

"We've been ordered to draw out the rebels," Captain Shaw announced after once again ordering me back behind the soldiers. "Let's show these rebels what a Union regiment can do."

We howled with delight as we stood, showing our solid, unbroken blue line. Three regiments aimed their rifles and unleashed a fierce volley at the cowering defenders. The rebels replied with shot and shell. The air seemed to buzz with the wasplike sounds of minié balls. The ground shook with the explosions of the rebels' heavy shells. One of the fort's big naval guns exploded. Its last shell landed fifty feet away, ripping a hole in the line and disabling a dozen or more soldiers.

I raced along the line, locating familiar faces and sighing with relief. Three soldiers of the Fifty-fifth were among the wounded, but no one was killed. Company C escaped unscathed.

Our firing drove the rebels back farther, allowing the Hundred and Thirteenth Illinois to creep up virtually to the edge of the fort. General Stuart asked Colonel Malmborg to supervise construction of a redoubt, a small fort to protect a battery of cannons. For a considerable time we waited in line, leaderless and without orders. The colonel, meanwhile, directed two hundred men from the Hundred and Twenty-seventh Illinois as they shoveled dirt into a make-shift earthwork.

All through the night we waited anxiously, anticipating a rebel counterattack or some new movement by our forces. We sat among stumps and underbrush, shivering with cold. No one had thought to bring our blankets and overcoats.

"You boys all right?" Chaplain Haney asked Lyston, Joe, and me.

"Yes, sir," I said, shaking as a fresh gust of wind blew through my ribs.

After he left, Lyston gripped my arm.

81

"Where's Pa?" he stammered.

I shuddered from a different kind of cold. I hadn't seen Pa in hours. I rose and walked quickly over to the chaplain.

"Captain Haney, have you seen Pa?" I asked.

"He's taken ill, Orion, but you shouldn't worry. The night air's hard on us old men."

"Hard on some of the young ones, too," I replied.

Bad as Lyston and I wanted to find Pa, we stayed put. We had our orders, after all. It was a trial, though, waiting and wondering all night.

Around daylight General Morgan's Thirteenth Corps arrived. We pulled back so that they could replace us with their superior numbers.

"Don't envy 'em, boys," Sergeant Curtiss said as we grumbled. "Whoever rushes that fort is going to bleed some."

We made our way to the right several hundred yards. Weary and dejected, we heard a familiar voice.

"Haven't you won the war yet?" General Sherman called, waving us toward a nearby field. "Whoever heard of rebels standing against good Ohio and Illinois men?"

We cheered him, and I think he was genuinely glad to be among us. It must have irked him, giving McClernand command, but he put that behind him and organized our attack. It was a long time coming. We advanced with a brisk step and took position between two batteries of artillery. We then faced the true trial of all soldiers—waiting.

An hour after midday orders finally arrived. The regiment was to attack three minutes after our artillery opened fire. Before the guns had finished, though, General Steele's men struck. The next thing I knew, General Sherman shouted for us to charge. The whole line rose and surged forward. The rebels in front of us held their works with stubborn determination. Twice their rifles and cannons drove us back. Finally we hugged the ground and let our artillery blast gaps in their lines.

The fighting continued for almost four hours. Impatient soldiers threw themselves forward in groups, and the fighting was hand to hand in places. The Fifty-fifth, being in the second line, contented itself with pinning the rebels to their trench. Gradually our artillery moved up into point-blank range, and we prepared to launch a final assault. Only moments before we were to charge, white flags appeared atop the fort's ramparts.

I was surprised at the rebels' sudden collapse. Once we had a chance to examine the fort, we saw what effective work the guns of our artillery and the gunboats had done. The heavy rebel emplacements were blasted into pieces. The big naval guns lay helpless on ruined carriages. The fort itself was a shambles, and many of the rebels were trembling from a mixture of cold and shock.

Not all the Confederates were ready to give up. A considerable number cursed their officers and swore that they had been betrayed. The loudest among them were a few companies of Texans. The ragged, underfed wretches gazed at us with rare hatred, and I couldn't help wincing.

"This isn't a gentle sort of war, Orion," Chaplain Haney told me later. "It won't be over very fast, either."

"No, sir," I replied. "I suppose not."

Lyston and I then headed out to where the surgeons had located the division hospital. Wounded and dying men lay in rows. I spotted some familiar faces, but I was glad that none of my closest friends were there. When I reached Pa, I felt my knees wobble. He was thin and gaunt, and he breathed with considerable difficulty.

"Pa?" I called.

"Orion, see to your brother," he replied. "It looks like I may have to pass some time in the hospital."

"You'll get well," I said, trying to bolster my courage as much as Pa's spirits.

"Winter's hard on us Howes," Pa added. "So watch out for yourself, too, son."

 NINE

We didn't remain long in Arkansas. Our engineers blew Fort Hindman to pieces. The Fifty-fifth Illinois was not one of the regiments selected to guard the prisoners or bury the dead. We marched back to the river and reembarked on the *Westmoreland*. By January 22 we had journeyed south down the Mississippi River to Young's Point, on the Louisiana side of the river and just north of the rebel forts guarding Vicksburg. We would remain there for some time.

Our journey was a solemn one. The cold nights without proper cover had spread sickness through the ranks. Pa was only one of the dozens of men coughing and aching below deck. Dr. Edward Roler, the regimental surgeon, did his best for the men, but it wasn't always enough. Those with the strength to get better recovered. The others didn't.

Lyston and I passed most of our time with Pa, bathing his feverish forehead and making him sip water. We helped with the other men, too. Dr. Roler ordered us out on deck from time to time. Otherwise, we stayed below.

I confess that the fresh air was welcome, but winter had brought a hard bite to the wind. The country on either side of the river had turned the same brownish gray as a reb's ragged uniform. Some of the sailors insisted that the Mississippi delta country was the finest in the whole nation, but I viewed it with disappointment. There may have been splendid homes and great plantations there once, but most of them had suffered. We frequently spied bare chimneys above river landings. Former slaves, abandoned by their rebel masters, waved at us from the shore. Sometimes we saw children fishing from the riverbanks. They glared at us defiantly or shouted insults.

"You can't take any of that to heart," Phil observed. "Those rebels who marched through Maryland last September likely found themselves every bit as welcome."

Young's Point proved to be a desolate place. The Fifty-fifth Illinois made its camp at the north end of the ill-fated Mississippi diversion canal. Back in July General Grant decided that one way to bypass Vicksburg was to dig a new channel for the Mississippi River. Contrabands dug a trench ten feet wide and six feet deep. It filled with water, but the Mississippi continued to surge along like before. The whole Fifteenth Corps, our regiment included, worked at widening the channel. Eventually we dug a canal close to fifty feet wide! The river still refused to shift its channel.

During those last days of January I had little to do. Captain Shaw decided that I was too frail to help with the digging, and the colonel ordered our serious sick cases transported to the hospital in Memphis. I remained under Dr. Roler's orders, but most of the time I sat and talked with Pa and Lyston.

"Don't you think Pa's better?" Lyston asked the first week of February.

"I hope so," I replied. To tell the truth, I believed Pa was growing worse. He always seemed tired, and he looked like he was aging quickly. Finally, on February 9, the doctor drew L and me aside.

"There's no point in your father suffering needlessly," Dr. Roler said. "He's trained the drummers, and we have no need of a band these days. I've recommended a discharge. My guess is that they'll send him to Memphis tomorrow."

"You youngsters ought to go along, see him home," Chaplain Haney added.

"I haven't served out my enlistment," I replied.

"Pa expects us to stay," Lyston added. "We're drummers, aren't we? You don't think just anyone can beat the calls, do you?"

Captain Shaw didn't think so. In fact, he told me pretty much that very thing.

"You can't leave just when the men are getting used to you," he scolded me. "I have nobody else I can rely on. Even poor Pitts, who had a try at drumming, isn't able."

I frowned. I had already seen Phil lying on a blanket a hundred feet away from the other wounded. I recognized the ugly red dots left by smallpox.

"You don't have to worry, Captain," I said. "I didn't come down here to leave the first chance I got. I'm no deserter. I plan to do my duty."

He nodded, touched the bill of his cap, and left.

Lyston and I went to see Pa together. I knew, despite what we had told Chaplain Haney, he would probably ask us to go home with him.

"You know they're discharging me, don't you?" he asked as we knelt beside his cot.

"Yes, sir," I answered. Lyston nodded.

"Captain Haney suggests you two go home as well. How do you feel about that?"

"I'm not sick," Lyston told him.

"Seems to me we haven't won the war yet, Pa," I added.

"Maybe we Howes have done our part, though," he said, coughing into a handkerchief. "Look around you. They're burying men older and stronger than you boys every day. I think I can convince Colonel Malmborg to let you go with me."

"Is that what you want us to do?" L asked.

"The question is, what do you want to do?" Pa argued. "Lyston, last winter was hard on you. Orion, no one's going to question your courage now. You've fought two battles. Our army will be a long time taking Vicksburg, and many a man will die doing it."

I gazed at Lyston, but he remained mute. Being older, I guessed it was for me to speak.

"Pa, Granny said that I was too young to join. It seems to me that if I go home now, I'll just be proving her right. If you only soldier when the going's easy, what sort of soldier does that make you?"

"Orry's right," L said, rising to his feet. "All our lives you've been telling us how important a drummer is. Now we're here, shouldn't we stay and do our jobs?"

"Yes," he said, surprising me. "If you have the heart to continue, stay and see the job done. Obey your officers, though, and don't take any unnecessary chances. Cordelia and I still expect you home when the fighting's over."

"You'll let us stay, then?" I asked.

"Once a man's old enough to join the ranks, he shouldn't

88

have to have his father's approval to do anything. You've grown tall, boys. Well, taller, anyway," he said, trying to conceal a smile. "Keep your spines straight and remember who you are. You write home and let me know how you are, too, or I'll come back here and—"

His words dissolved into an outburst of coughing then, and we tried to make him more comfortable. We stayed with him until Doc Roler chased us to our beds. We were back the next morning to carry him aboard a transport bound for Memphis.

With Pa gone, I devoted most of my time to cheering Phil. Being raised in a town and schooled in Chicago, I had the benefit of immunization against smallpox. I showed the scar on my arm to Dr. Roler, and he allowed me to sit with my feverish friend. I would feed Phil broth, see he drank plenty of good water, and try to entertain him with a song or a game of cards.

"Strange state of affairs, Orry," Phil told me one morning. "I expected to be looking after you."

"You did it for five months," I reminded him. "It's my turn."

"Well, you'll be finished here soon. There's a battle coming, and the company's sure to need you. You stay close to Johnny and Henry Curtiss. They're steady, and they'll see you through the worst."

"Until you get over this," I replied.

Phil looked at me solemnly. He didn't say anything, but I watched his eyes get strange. He finally managed a little bit of a smile, and he squeezed my hand.

"You've been a good friend, Orry," he told me. "Now go get some rest and leave me to do the same."

I started to argue, but his eyes were close to pleading. I walked over to Dr. Roler, but he was busy. Instead, I played cards with Joe and Lyston until we grew weary enough to go to sleep.

Phil Pitts died sometime that night, the fourteenth day of February 1863. We buried him the next morning on a little rise overlooking the river. I don't think I was ever again able to be as cheerful a soldier.

Before February came to an end, we had plenty of reasons for hating Young's Point. Our regiment, already understrength, lost men there to every imaginable ailment. Even those who stood at roll call suffered from chills and fevers. One night as Lyston and I spread our blankets at the far end of the shelter Joe Edwards had helped us make, I heard something slither past my toe.

"Ayyyy!" Lyston cried.

"Look out, Joe!" I shouted as he started to stomp on it.

Joe jumped back in the nick of time. A copperhead raced by only inches from his toe.

"Whew!" he gasped, shaking his head. "Here I thought they were all back home, stirring up trouble."

"Could be worse," Sergeant Curtiss told me when I reported the snake. "The Fifty-fourth Ohio had a man bit by a cottonmouth. Snake crawled into his blankets and clamped on to his neck. Died ten minutes later."

"The man or the snake?" I asked, hoping to lighten the moment.

"Knowing those Ohio boys, it was probably both," the sergeant replied.

We hoped that better weather would arrive in March, but we were disappointed again. True, it wasn't as cold, but the rains came and stayed. The river rose dangerously close to the levees, and we passed several afternoons piling dirt up to protect our camp. Some enterprising rebels took note of our peril and began breaking the levees. On March 7 I awoke to find water swirling around my feet.

"L!" I shouted. I jumped up and slammed my forehead against the roof of our shelter. Lyston blinked his eyes awake as water swept over his legs. I helped him to his knees, and we did our best to collect soggy blankets. I had to make a mad dash to catch my drum before it floated away.

Outside, what remained of the regiment splashed around, rescuing what they could. If a company of rebs had appeared, they might have captured our entire unit. We didn't have a single rifle with dry powder.

"I've seen all manner of rebel tricks, but this is the straw that broke the camel's back," Sergeant Curtiss howled. "They've gone and turned the Fifty-fifth into a regiment of amphibians!"

Those next few days we looked back fondly on our old snake- and insect-ravaged camp. For miles you couldn't find a patch of dry ground big enough to support a dog tent. We prayed for the chance to march into the countryside, attack another rebel fort, or even charge the powerful batteries at Vicksburg. We felt so helpless, lying in the Louisiana mud, staring at the campfires across the river.

On March 11 we finally had something to cheer about. The rebel batteries woke us with the sounds of a furious bombardment. The navy, it turned out, had taken an old river barge and disguised it to look like one of our ironclad gunboats. Huge logs, painted black to resemble naval guns, poked menacingly out of sham gunports. The rebel gunners, staring at the shadowy monster in the dim light, peppered it with cannonballs, which naturally sailed through its painted canvas sides and exploded harmlessly in the river beyond.

The next morning we got a closer look at the thing. Some Company B men happened to be on picket duty when the barge drifted ashore. Two hogsheads wrapped in black canvas passed for smokestacks. Kettles of boiling tar provided the smoke. A pair of mock wheelhouses carried messages for the rebels. The words were enough to make a river rat blush!

It was far too good a joke to let die in the shallows off Young's Point. We collected some long tree branches and eventually redirected the phantom ironclad into the strong current produced by the river channel near the entrance of our canal. Magically the mock monster swung out into deeper water.

As was usually the case, a heavy fog clung to the river that morning. As the sun began to burn away the haze, rebel gunners on the far shore at Warrenton glimpsed our spook ship and opened fire. A few weeks earlier, rebels had captured one of our rams, *Queen of the West*. The ram, seeing the fire of the batteries fail to stop our ghost ship, raised anchor and hurried to where the rebels were working at repairing the partially sunken *Indianola*, a powerful Union ironclad. The rebels hoped to use the *Indianola* to defend Vicksburg. In a fit of panic, the rebels stopped their work, boarded *Queen of the West*, and blew up the *Indianola*.

Thereafter, the Fifty-fifth boasted to be the only regiment in the army to have sunk a rebel ironclad. The navy, naturally, claimed all the credit, and we got no mention in the

92

official reports. Those of us who witnessed it knew what happened, though.

We were still celebrating the *Indianola*'s destruction when the army paymaster arrived. No one in the regiment had been paid since November. I took my place at the end of Company C's meager line and waited my turn. The twenty-six dollars I'd received in Memphis back in November hadn't lasted long. I wasn't well equipped for soldiering, and between buying better shoes and underwear, the money had vanished. This time I received fifty-two dollars. Lyston and I agreed to send twenty-five each home to Pa. We owed debts here and there, too. L had torn the brim off his cap, and he had to buy a new one. I bought needles and some thread to repair tears in my shirt and trousers. We had just enough left to buy new boots. With our camp gradually sinking into Mississippi goo, that was money well spent.

No sooner had we spent our money than orders arrived for us to board the *Von Phul*, a transport.

"At last, we're going to attack Vicksburg," Henry declared.

But instead of steaming south toward the city, we headed upriver. Contrabands had betrayed the location of hidden stores of rebel supplies, and we set about collecting them. In all we located five thousand bales of cotton, scores of hogs, nine hundred head of cattle, and considerable quantities of corn and sugar. It was truly wonderful, watching the distraught faces of planters when we carted off the cotton. Each bale was stamped *Property of C. S. A*—Confederate States of America. To our dismay, sailors later added *Captured by the U.S. Navy*. We learned afterward that the ship

93

captains received prize money for that cotton! We did all the work and got nothing while those boatmen received pay for nothing.

Needless to say, the petition men went to work on our grievance. Nothing came of it, though, and we sailed back down the river to Milliken's Bend, a big supply point on the Louisiana side of the river. We hoped to camp there, above the broken levees. Instead, Colonel Malmborg explained that we had orders to march south to our old camp at Young's Point.

We were still at Young's Point when April arrived, marking the beginning of the war's third year. No one could have imagined in the days following Fort Sumter that we were embarking on such a long, costly, destructive war. Our own growing impatience had its counterpart in Washington. Changes were coming.

On April 4 Major General Frank P. Blair arrived with orders to assume command of the Second Division, Fifteenth Army Corps. That was David Stuart's command, and our former colonel responded angrily to the news. The Senate, we learned, took heed of our complaints and refused to confirm his promotion to general. Stuart resigned from the army and went home to Illinois. It was fair to say the regiment as a whole was happy to see the last of him.

There were others who would have liked to go along.

"I wonder why they don't let privates resign?" Rienzi Cleveland asked.

"You know full well why," Joe replied. "There'd be nobody left to do the fighting."

Once General Blair took charge, we noticed several changes. Our officers had always suspected Stuart of mis-

94

managing things. General Blair saw to it that promotions were handed out promptly, and we were paid on April 11, exactly on time. Two days later the general held a grand review of his division. We drummers led the regimental parade, playing "Battle Cry of Freedom" as the men sang the rousing words.

"It does my heart good to hear you put your feelings into words," the general told us. "Soon we'll be marching under the banner of freedom against the very demons who would enslave forever their fellow men."

The general's words were still ringing in our ears when Admiral David Porter led his fleet of eight gunboats past the Vicksburg batteries April 16. The transport *Henry Clay* exploded in a fiery torrent, but no one aboard died. Only eight men received wounds.

"Admiral Porter's proved he can run past the rebel batteries," Henry told me. "We'll soon board transports and move across the river. I'll bet Vicksburg's ours before June."

I should have accepted the wager. We were a long way from ready to cross the river, and Vicksburg still had plenty of teeth with which to strike. We did assemble as a division on April 21, but it wasn't to hear that orders for an attack had been issued. Instead, the Adjutant General of the whole army, Lorenzo Thomas, had come to speak concerning the merits of arming contrabands and enlisting them in the army.

General Thomas stood in the bed of an army wagon. He explained how, in his opinion, it was only sensible to allow former slaves to bear arms against their former masters. Why shouldn't black men, Thomas asked, be allowed to join in the armed struggle that stood to benefit them the most? Should the Confederacy prevail, was it not the very freedom of the black man that stood at risk?

General Sherman also spoke that day. He had spent the final months before the war teaching in a Louisiana military college. Northern newspapers had questioned his loyalty, his competence, and even his sanity. Anyone who saw him on his horse at Arkansas Post would have recognized the wound done his pride by placing McClernand in command of what everyone viewed as Sherman's corps.

"Men," Sherman began, "you all know me." We did, indeed. He reminded us of his steadfast refusal to return fugitive slaves despite the demands of local landowners and public officials. He spoke of his belief that the same men employed in the army as cooks and teamsters could serve ably as soldiers.

The Second Division, being mainly Illinois and Ohio men, received the speech well. Afterward we formed as regiments and voted on the proposal.

"What do you think, Johnny?" Henry asked his brother as the three of us began passing out ballots.

"I think we're going to need soldiers to win this war," Sergeant Curtiss declared. "The state's paying bounties to recruits, but we still can't find enough men to restore the Fifty-fifth to full strength. Give the blacks rifles and able leaders. They can stand and die as well as anyone."

"What about you, Orry?" Henry then asked.

I scratched my head. I wasn't used to offering opinions, especially on important matters. I pondered it a moment before speaking.

"I think the generals are right," I told them. "They've got more at stake than anybody, so they ought to be allowed to fight. Remember how they came to us and told about the hidden cotton?"

"But can you trust a black man to hold your flank?" Henry asked. "When all they've ever been taught to do is fear their masters?"

"I believe I'd trust 'em above most of those Copperhead boys from downstate," the sergeant argued. "You wait and see if I'm not right."

He was, too. In June a brigade of Texans attacked the supply base at Milliken's Bend. The three regiments of the newly recruited African Brigade guarding the stores fought stubbornly, holding off the rebels until gunboats arrived to break up the attack. Of the 652 men our army lost in the battle, 566 were members of the African Brigade. The few black prisoners were enslaved once more.

 TEN

From the end of April on into the first days of May, the Fifty-fifth Illinois marched up and down the west bank of the Mississippi in a series of feints designed to deceive the Confederate defenders of Vicksburg. After our successful attack on Fort Hindman, the rebels couldn't know for certain where we might go or what we might do. I wondered myself.

Those were trying days for me. Lyston and I had received a letter from Pa a week or so before, saying he had reached home safely, but now that we were moving around, the mail never caught up with us. We wrote Pa, Granny, even Cordelia, but without getting an answer. We didn't know what to think.

"They probably wonder if we're still alive," Lyston told me.

"Our letters probably arrive," I argued. "It's just difficult for them to get word to us."

"I know," Lyston said, frowning. "Doesn't make it easier, though."

No, it didn't. We were both a hair homesick that spring. It

was even worse for me because with Phil dead, I didn't even have anyone to pair my shelter half with. The older fellows shied away from us youngsters. That was fine so long as Captain Shaw allowed me to tent with Lyston and Joe. But once we set out from camp again, I'd be all alone. Eventually Henry Curtiss invited me to join him.

"I just wish we'd get on with it, whatever it is," Henry told me the night we arrived at Milliken's Bend. His brother Johnny only laughed.

"Why do you figure all these stores are piled here?" he asked. "Why are the generals all sleeping on the transports? It's not so they can attack Little Rock. We'll be marching on Vicksburg any day now."

Rumors of other campaigns drifted through camp, but I had to agree with the sergeant. Almost daily another steamer or gunboat arrived. You didn't need a fleet to sail up the Arkansas River.

By May 3 our whole brigade was encamped near Milliken's Bend. The Fifty-fifth Illinois, being closest to the landing, had the first chance to spy a group of officers leaving a supply ship.

"Look there," Joe called. "It's the general!"

True enough, General Morgan Smith, still limping along on crutches because of his wound, had come to visit. Our officers quickly surrounded him, but the general went right through them.

"I didn't come out here to see you officers," General Smith announced. "How are you boys?"

We cheered him loudly. In an instant he was among us, touching a hand here and there, asking how we had been.

"Sick, mostly," Michael Ainsbury, one of our corporals,

said. "This swamp's no place to camp, sir. When are we going after the rebs at Vicksburg?"

"I'd tell you boys to leave strategy to us," the general replied, "but you wouldn't listen." We laughed. "You'll get a chance to fight soon. I promise you that."

We headed south the next day, and on May 5 Governor Richard Yates of Illinois visited us at Richmond, Louisiana.

"Sorry we're not in that other Richmond," he told us. "The one the rebs have turned into their capital. We'll be there soon, though."

We held a grand review for the governor. Afterward, he paid a call on Colonel Malmborg.

"I heard a bit of it," Joe told Lyston and me later. "Governor Yates is worried about trade. He says the farmers upriver need to ship their crops down to New Orleans and then off to Europe. Vicksburg's blocking the way."

It turned out that the delay in taking control of the Mississippi River was one reason the Copperheads were growing stronger. With President Lincoln coming up for reelection next year, it seemed more important than ever to capture Vicksburg.

"Vicksburg's the key," the governor told us. "The president himself said it. With that city in our hands, the Confederacy's cut in half. The whole interior of the South is open to invasion. We've got to have it, boys. What do you say? Can you take her?"

We cheered and tossed our hats. Given half a chance, we'd smash the rebels and capture the place.

The following day we turned south and marched with new purpose. We covered fifteen miles a day until we reached Hard Times, Louisiana, south of Vicksburg, on May 11. Steamboats ferried us across the river to the Mississippi shore. Then we marched northward in order to strike the rebels at Vicksburg from the rear.

There was a new sense of urgency to our movements. We could hear the distant rumble of cannons. The army's vanguard was already fighting. As we marched through Grand Gulf and Port Gibson those next days, we passed broken wagons and small camps of wounded. Sometimes a column of weary, ragged rebel prisoners passed on the opposite side of the road.

Nothing prepared us for the sight of the little town of Raymond, though. What might have once been a peaceful country town had become a sea of graves and hospital tents. The rebels had put up quite a fight, but we had driven them from the field in the end. All that remained was the aftermath of battle—the suffering and dying. Flies buzzed around a stack of rags to the right of the road. Only when we got closer did I realize that it was a pile of amputated arms and legs.

"Eyes to the front!" Sergeant Curtiss shouted, and I did my best to stare at the dusty road ahead. I drummed a steady beat. But each time I inhaled, the smell of death overwhelmed me. I fought the urge to be sick. My fingers gripped the sticks tighter.

"It's all right, son," Captain Shaw said, easing me off to the side of the road. "It hits every one of us now and then."

I gazed up at him a moment. Then my stomach turned, and I ran over to a ditch and became ill. I wasn't alone. Others joined me.

101

Beyond Raymond the country was scarred by creeks and small rivers. The armies had clashed there as well. We came across fences and buildings splintered by rifle fire. We passed dead horses and mules. Surely a great battle was in the offing. As the army spread out across the countryside, I realized our regiment would soon be fighting, too.

On May 17 we saw our first action. The Fifty-fifth Illinois led the rest of General Morgan Smith's brigade toward the Big Black River. Wagons carrying a long rubber pontoon bridge followed, and we expected to use it to cross the river. The rebels had other ideas. They had placed a small earthwork on the far bank, guarding the best crossing. Riflemen stationed there could hit anyone approaching the river. Colonel Malmborg ordered two companies to form a skirmish line, and soon we were exchanging volleys with the rebels.

It was about that time that General Blair appeared. He studied the progress of our skirmishers and shook his head.

"This won't do," he announced. He rode his horse to where Colonel Malmborg stood, and the two officers discussed the problem. The general issued orders, and Colonel Malmborg directed Company C to move downstream, swim the river, and take the earthwork from its unprotected flank.

Captain Shaw told me to beat assembly. He then explained the plan.

"Strip down to your trousers and follow me," he commanded, and we kicked off our shoes and unbuttoned our shirts.

"A fine way to fight," Rienzi Cleveland grumbled. "Next thing you know he'll order us to charge Vicksburg naked!"

Before we could mount our flank attack, General Sherman rode up. He immediately countermanded our orders. Instead, he brought up a battery and had the gunners place their cannons in the shelter of an outbuilding. The artillerymen quickly placed their guns, and after a few shots, the rebels raised a white flag from their earthwork.

Captain Lucien Crooker of Company F and eight of his men rowed across the river on a pontoon and took possession of the rebels—a young lieutenant and ten soldiers. The remainder of the regiment paddled over, and we spread out in a crescent to protect the crossing. We waited anxiously while the engineers assembled the bridge. They finished at dusk, and regiments of our army began crossing. All night men moved westward while we stood watch. Except for some gunfire exchanged near a railroad bridge, we had little trouble from the rebels.

That next morning Sergeant Curtiss woke me even earlier than usual.

"Beat assembly," he told me. "We're advancing again."

I opened and closed my fingers, hoping to start the blood flowing. I yawned away my weariness and tapped out reveille. The men responded with grumbles, and one even threw his shoe at me. Fortunately, it missed. I was too tired to duck.

"Get up, boys!" Sergeant Curtiss yelled. "We've got a war to win."

They remained sluggish until Captain Shaw marched over and began whacking the sleepyheads on their rumps with the flat of his sword. The captain's fiery eyes warned that next time the sword might do some slicing.

For my part, I managed to get dressed and beat assembly fast enough to satisfy the officers. I was hungry, though, and the rations we had cooked at Raymond were gone.

"Have we time to eat breakfast, Johnny?" Henry asked.

"Not even to cook it," the sergeant replied. "Prepare to follow Company B. We'll eat supper. Maybe."

Over the next several hours, we covered better than twelve miles. It was exhausting work, marching through that hilly country in the Mississippi heat. I felt as if an inch of dirt and dust clung to me. My throat ached, and my lips were dry as a desert. For the first time I could remember, my legs ached, and I had trouble keeping up with the soldiers.

"We going to take a rest, Captain?" Rienzi Cleveland finally asked.

"You see any other company falling out of line?" Captain Shaw replied. "Well?"

"Those other fellows aren't human beings if they're not tired," Corporal Ainsbury argued. "Little Howe there's about to collapse, and I'm not going to be far behind."

"You need a rest, Howe?" Captain Shaw asked.

"I wouldn't mind one," I answered.

"Then I suppose we'd best have one," the captain said. "We can't go on without our drummer."

I knew he was having a laugh at my expense, but I didn't care. I was too tired.

The rest of the regiment saw us pause. Soon they, too, interrupted their march. Men sipped water from their canteens and chewed a bit of dried beef or stale biscuit. It was an amazing thing, that brief rest. It revived us, and we continued our march with renewed vigor.

By two o'clock we could see the outline of the impressive rebel outer works. Beyond them we saw Vicksburg. The landward approach seemed no more vulnerable to attack than did the high bluffs overlooking the river. Cannons crowned the hillside redoubts. Battle flags marked the locations of dozens of veteran regiments.

"They must have ten thousand men manning that line," Captain Shaw said. His voice betrayed his concern, and I shuddered. If the officers were afraid, what chance did the rest of us have to muster our courage?

General Smith ordered our brigade forward. Skirmishers moved out in front. They exchanged shots with the rebel pickets, but little came of that. The rebels simply moved back into their works, leaving our men with the choice of withdrawing or facing the massed force occupying the surrounding hills.

"Look there," Henry said, nudging my arm.

To my right generals Sherman and Grant rode with their staffs. The generals pointed to the right and then to the left. Clearly, they were planning an attack. We soldiers couldn't guess their thoughts. We sat down and stared at the mighty fortress the rebs had made of Vicksburg. To the north lay the Chickasaw Bluff and the line of works that had stymied our earlier effort. Soldiers wearing blue now took possession of that position.

"That's good news," Henry told me.

"What?" I asked.

"The navy can get our supplies to us up the Yazoo. We'll have something to eat again."

Now I have to confess that while there wasn't all that much of me in those days, just eighty-five pounds, what there was ached for food. Some of the older men openly grumbled about the lack of provisions. When the first supply wagons rumbled over from Chickasaw Bluff, we went wild.

That afternoon the generals eased us forward, regiment by regiment. The Fifty-fifth Illinois took up position alongside a narrow track, the Graveyard Road. I couldn't imagine a more ominous name.

We passed that night in a cornfield within musket range of the formidable rebel works. Company F advanced closest and formed a picket line. From time to time rebel sharpshooters would fire, and Company F replied. We had two men hit during the night, but my company escaped harm.

I don't know that I would have slept well even if everything had been quiet. I was full of foreboding. The night air was heavy, and clouds cast eerie shadows across the moon.

"Orry?" Lyston called to me shortly after midnight.

"L?" I replied.

"I guess you can't sleep, either," he said as he crawled over beside me. "I feel strange."

"I know," I said, letting him slide under my arm the way he had when he was younger. "We've been through this before, though. I don't suppose it will be any different."

"It *feels* different," he told me. "I was nervous the night before the rebels attacked us at Shiloh. I didn't know why. It's the same now."

"You think they'll attack in the morning?" I asked.

"No," he said, sighing. "We will."

"You can't be sure."

"I'm no military genius, Orry, but I heard the colonel

talking to the captains. Grant doesn't believe the rebs have their line fully manned. He figures there will be a weak spot here and there. We'll probe until we find it."

"There's no weak spot in front of us," I said, shuddering. In spite of the May heat, I felt cold.

"That's how it looks to me, too," Joe Edwards said, joining us. "Unless we're wrong, there won't be too many of us left this time tomorrow."

It was a chilling thought. I believed it was completely possible, too. Maybe that's why I walked to the supply wagon and snatched a fresh loaf of bread. I then made my way through the regiment until I located Company C. I gave a piece of bread to every soldier still awake. That was most of them, too.

"Thanks, Howe," Captain Shaw said when I handed him a hunk. "You better get some rest, though."

"You, too," I said.

I gave the last of the bread to Rienzi Cleveland. He took it, smiled, and passed two letters to me.

"One for Ma and Pa," he explained. "The other's for Adrian, my brother. He's seventeen now and will likely want to join the army. It's just a word or two or help him get through."

"Scared?" I asked.

"Not scared," he said, gazing toward the distant pinpricks of light that marked the rebel lines. "Just prepared."

"Why give 'em to me?" I asked.

"They'll leave you in back, Orry, with the other boys. You'll have a better chance there."

I hung my head. I wasn't eager to join the front rank, but I

107

hated the notion that all my friends thought that I wouldn't be sharing their risks.

"Maybe—" I started to say.

"You stay back there, too, Orry," Rienzi scolded. "Only a man with a rifle will do any good up front. Later, when we're shot, you'll be a help."

"Sure," I muttered.

 ELEVEN

Morning found the Fifty-fifth Illinois in that same cornfield along the Graveyard Road. Colonel Malmborg sent companies A and B up to the picket line to relieve the weary men of Company F. He then made his way through the ranks, offering encouragement and promising us rations. Actually, we got very little to eat. After the initial load provided by the navy, little had arrived.

It didn't matter to me. I had no appetite. My stomach churned, and I couldn't have held a knife steady if all the world depended on it.

I envied the boys in Company G. They moved off in support of the Chicago Board of Trade battery A, a short distance to our left.

"I wish we'd go ahead and attack," I told Henry.

"In a hurry to get killed?" he asked.

"Not particularly. It's just that the worrying is worse than the danger."

"Trust me, Orry, it isn't," Henry assured me. "You can't imagine how bad it's going to be."

"Worse'n Shiloh," Rienzi said. "Worse by a far sight."

Shortly before two o'clock we were ordered to form ranks. Three volleys of artillery fire would signal an advance all across the front.

"The rebs can't hold us everywhere," Captain Shaw asserted. "It's a reasonable way to find the weak spot."

The trouble was I still didn't see any weak spots. The rebels held the high ground, with every advantage of vision and concealment. We had to charge blindly up narrow lanes swept by their artillery. It had the earmark of a massacre.

I jumped when the cannons unleashed their first volley. I tried to think of a prayer, but nothing came to mind.

"Howe, you go on back to the chaplain now," Captain Shaw said as he took the measure of the men. "Stay back there, too."

I did as ordered. Chaplain Haney instructed us to wrap white cloths around our arms. We would remain in the corn-field while the fighting went on.

"We'll see to the wounded later, once the shooting's died down."

I remained restless. Joe and Lyston tried to calm me, but I was worried about my friends. The second volley started a tremor of anticipation, and the third started an avalanche of men rushing toward the Vicksburg line.

It was even worse than I expected. The ground was broken by tree stumps and fallen trees. The men found it impossible to maintain their line, and soldiers broke off in twos and threes. As they got within a hundred yards of the rebels, the graycoats rose and unleashed a vicious volley. It was as if a sheet of solid flame swept the hills. One minute hundreds of men raced along. The next minute three out of four lay wounded or dying. Those who continued were killed by a second volley.

It was a terrible thing to behold. As regiments continued their individual attacks, assaults lost their vigor. Soldiers stumbled along, firing their rifles wildly at the invisible enemy. Cannons tried to blast gaps in the rebel defenses. As our own men advanced, though, our artillery had to cease fire for fear of hitting Union soldiers.

The rebel cannons had no similar problem. They blasted our soldiers as they heroically tried to scale walls and capture parapets. Other rebel guns fired into our supporting lines. One shell rocked the earth ten yards to my right, and another blew two Ohio men to pieces a stone's throw to my left.

"We can't just stay here," I told Lyston.

"We can, too," he argued.

"Look, we've got wounded out there," I said, pointing to a pair of Company A soldiers.

"All right, but we're coming right back."

I started off in the lead, but a shell exploded in my path, and I hugged the earth. Lyston settled in beside me, and neither of us went another inch. Then I glimpsed a couple of Ohio drummers helping a soldier to the rear. I took a deep breath and continued.

I stumbled along fifty feet or so before reaching the first soldier. I'm not sure who it was. His face was pale, and he bled from two holes in his chest.

"Don't take it to heart, boy," he told me. "I never expected to get very old."

111

I continued on even as the supporting regiments on either side of the Fifty-fifth Illinois gave way. Colonel Malmborg kept up his own advance anyway. Soon, though, the rebels had us in a trap. We were exposed on three sides, and they peppered our ranks with rifle and cannon fire.

"Go back!" I heard Captain Shaw shout as I rushed toward Company C. "Go back!"

Wounded men lay there, though, and I considered it my job to try and help them. I climbed over a stump and found three terribly wounded soldiers. Corporal James Curry of Company D bled from a gaping chest wound. Corporal Jim Gay, who carried our flag, bled from a wound in his shoulder. A third corporal, Joe Deems of Company A, lay in a pool of blood. A ball had sliced through his thigh.

"Here," Joe Edwards said, handing me a dressing. "Plug that shoulder."

I held a bandage against Deems's shoulder while Joe applied the binding. We managed to get Deems and Gay back to Surgeon Roler. Curry was past saving.

"Wait, Orry," Lyston pleaded when Joe and I turned back toward the fighting. "I'll go with you."

"You stay and help the doctor," I advised. "Joe and I'll bring in the wounded."

As we crept across the battlefield, we located few men who remained alive. The survivors had taken cover behind a low rise. They desperately dueled with the rebel sharpshooters. As I approached, Sergeant Curtiss ordered me back.

"You'll do us no good here, Howe!" he shouted. "See if you can get some ammunition to us, though. We're almost out."

"Here's some," Joe said, taking a cartridge box off a dead man.

I examined another man and found he had four unused cartridges. Joe and I then scrambled around, emptying the boxes of the dead until we had close to fifty cartridges. We raced toward our friends, but a rebel volley drove us to cover. Joe rose a moment later, only to be struck down by a minié ball.

"Orry?" he called.

I dragged him to safety. Tears flooded my eyes as I tore his shirt open. Fortunately, the wound was in his shoulder. It appeared to be a clean one, too. The ball had gone through the fleshy part and passed through without hitting any bone.

"Don't worry," I told him. "I'll get you back."

I managed to get a dressing in place and bind it tightly. I then got Joe on his feet and helped him to the rear.

"Joe?" Chaplain Haney cried when we arrived at the makeshift hospital in back of the cornfield. "Orry, you stay here now. Joe here's proof of the danger."

"Can't, sir," I answered. "The men are low on cartridges. I'm going to find them some."

All of a sudden my fear passed. It was as if everything was in sharp focus. I had to collect cartridges off the dead and wounded. I had to save my desperate comrades. At first I had little trouble gathering up cartridge boxes. Other men started doing the same thing, though, and soon only the men lying in clear view of the rebels had ammunition. I made a run toward two dead soldiers, and a dozen rifles opened fire on me. One tore a hole in my shirt and a second nicked the heel of my left boot. I grabbed the cartridge box, but to my disgust, it was empty.

"That's enough of that!" Captain Shaw complained when I crawled to his side.

"Dis von't do," Colonel Malmborg agreed. "Ve need much, much more. You go back, Howe, and tell dem dat ve need ammunition. If ve have none, ve vill all die."

"He's not going alone," Captain Shaw insisted. "I need a volunteer—"

"I'll go," Rienzi said, forcing a smile onto his face. He crawled over, gave me a slap on the back, and rose. A rebel ball slammed into his shoulder, and he fell against me, bleeding.

"I told you," Captain Shaw grumbled as he helped pull Rienzi off me. "You should have done what I asked and stayed back. Now—"

"We'll take him, Captain," Corporal Ainsbury volunteered. "Babcock, Hamer, and me."

I nodded at the three. Orin Babcock was a smallish fellow, barely eighteen, and as fine a cardplayer as there was in the regiment. Our names being similar, I had tried to kindle a friendship, but he preferred gambling with the sergeants, who had enough money to make a game interesting. Bob Hamer was a hair past twenty, taller, and the sort who keeps to himself.

"Get through," Captain Shaw urged.

"Get dem to send us five hundred rounds!" Colonel Malmborg shouted. "And remember, calibre 54!"

Those final words echoed through my mind as I prepared to commence my race down the Graveyard Road. Our rate of fire had dropped dangerously, and the rebels paused, as if knowing something important was about to happen.

114

Corporal Ainsbury chose that instant to rise, and I jumped up and raced off. Rebel sharpshooters took aim and began firing.

Corporal Ainsbury uttered a weak cry and fell. A single minié ball had struck his left temple and torn through his brain. I started to turn back, but Babcock dragged me along.

"Oh," he said when a rebel ball crashed into his head below the left ear. He fell first to his knees and then to the earth. I wanted to check on him, too, but Hamer waved for me to come on. I ran for all my life across the low hills toward the safety of the cornfield. We must have run half a mile when Hamer, too, fell. An eagle-eyed rebel had shot him through the head.

I instinctively threw myself behind a fallen tree and prayed it would all be over. The old terror returned. We four had left together, and now there was only me.

"The men," I reminded myself. "They'd risk their lives for you. They've done it lots of times."

I rose and raced toward the cornfield. The rebels fired slowly, deliberately, but their weapons had no power over me. Sure, I fell once or twice, but no ounce of lead was going to hurt me. Then, suddenly, a fiery heat sliced through my right thigh, and I fell. When I ran my fingers up my leg, I felt something warm and sticky—blood.

Fool, I told myself. They got you after all.

I probed for the ball with my fingers, but it wasn't there. It had passed cleanly through! I laughed a moment, relieved that I wasn't doomed to die on that field as my companions had. Then I scrambled to my feet and stumbled on.

Before, I heard nothing. Now, though, hundreds of eyes

seemed to follow my every movement. Voices cheered me. I didn't want their cheers, though. I wanted a warm bed, a good supper, and some rest.

Somehow, magically, I escaped further harm. I couldn't believe the rebels didn't hit me. I dragged my right leg like a fifty-pound weight as I struggled on toward the cornfield. Each time I looked down, it appeared worse. Blood continued to ooze from the wicked tear in my flesh. I was beginning to feel faint. I nevertheless managed to limp to our lines.

"Orry, you've gone and gotten yourself shot!" Lyston exclaimed, clutching my side.

"Boy, we'd best dress that," Dr. Roler added.

"Not yet," I pleaded. "I have to send ammunition to the men."

"Orry, wait!" Chaplain Haney called.

I continued on up the road, though. For several minutes I searched for an ordnance sergeant. Finding none, I went on. By that point my right leg was nearly covered with blood. I desperately needed to find someone in charge. That's when I saw him—William T. Sherman himself. I stumbled over and shouted.

"General, sir!"

"Yes?" Sherman replied.

"General Sherman, send some cartridges to Colonel Malmborg. The men are all out."

"What is the matter, my boy?" the general asked.

"They shot me in the leg, sir," I told him. "But I can go to the hospital. Send the cartridges right away."

And then a shell crashed nearby, and I flinched. Sherman simply smiled.

"I'll attend to the cartridges, son," the general promised. "You get yourself to the rear."

I started to limp on toward the division hospital, but suddenly I recalled the colonel's final words.

"General, send them calibre 54!" I yelled. "Calibre 54!"

 TWELVE

Up to that moment, I really never knew what pain felt like. Maybe I was too scared or just too busy to feel anything. Suddenly it came over me like a wave. I tried to manage another step, but my leg wouldn't move. My stomach tied itself in a knot, and I doubled over.

"What's wrong, boy?" an Ohio soldier asked.

"Mmmy leg," I stammered.

"He's bleeding," the Ohioan observed. "John, Mitch, let's get him along to the surgeons."

They picked me up in their powerful arms, and I closed my eyes. I felt for a time as if I were floating over the battlefield. I refused to hear the thunder of the cannonade. I shut out the cries of the wounded.

"There he is," I heard Lyston cry. "Those three soldiers are carrying him."

I cracked my eye open and saw Lyston. Henry was with him.

"I'll take the lad," Henry told the Ohio boys. They set me down, and Henry took charge of me. "You've grown heavy," Henry told me. "If you keep acquiring lead, you'll have to find someone else to carry you."

I tried to smile, but my thigh was throbbing, and I just couldn't manage it. Lyston touched my hand. I wanted to cheer him, but I was too tired. I closed my eyes again.

I passed from the real world into something akin to a cloud. I wasn't exactly asleep. I heard voices, and I felt pain. Later something cold and hot at the same time seemed to tear at my wound, and I passed into unconsciousness. When I awoke, it was dark outside. I lay on a blanket in the parlor of a small house.

"You had us worried," Dr. Roler said, patting my shoulder. "Whatever were you thinking, running across that field with the whole rebel army shooting at you!"

"I—"

"He wasn't thinking," Lyston said. The sight of my worried little brother sitting beside me chased some of the fog from my head, and I managed a brief grin.

"Well, we'd best let you rest," the surgeon said, touching my forehead to check for fever. "You've lost a lot of blood, son. You won't be fighting any battles for some time to come."

I nodded. Once the surgeon had gone, I eased my right arm down along my side. I couldn't erase the memory of the pile of arms and legs at Raymond, and I had to know whether I was still a two-legged human. The first sensation was one of surprise. I was naked beneath my blanket!

"L, my clothes," I mumbled.

"They had to cut them off," he explained. "The blood—"

"They did the same to me," a familiar voice called from

119

behind me. I rolled over and stared into Joe Edwards's amused eyes.

"You all right, Joe?" I asked, sighing with relief as I touched my knee. The leg was still there.

"I won't do any drumming for a time," he answered. His shoulder was heavily bandaged, and he was pale as death. "You?"

"I've been better," I said, taking a deep breath. "The others? Rienzi? Henry?"

"Henry carried you here," Lyston reminded me. "Close to a mile in all. Rienzi's around here somewhere."

"His arm's bandaged, but he's walking around, helping with the other wounded," Joe said. "We had twenty-four men hit. Eight of them died."

I recalled Corporal Ainsbury. Jim Curry. Babcock and Hamer.

Captain Shaw appeared then, and I tried to salute. He eased my arm down halfway through.

"I told you we needed our drummer," the captain said, sliding back the blanket so that he could see my bandaged leg. "Now who's going to rouse the men?"

"Sergeant Curtiss will just have to shout louder," I suggested.

"There aren't all that many left to wake," Lyston added. "We have a few drummers, though."

"I'm sorry I couldn't stay back," I added. "We had wounded men out there. I had to try and help."

"And is that why you ran across the field?" the captain asked.

"No, sir," I said, sighing. "I guess it was because the men seemed so desperate. When I brought them cartridges, I felt like a real part of the company. You needed me. It was a stupid thing to do, I suppose, but I'm only a boy. We don't always show much sense."

"Well, it was the bravest thing I ever saw in all my life, Orry," Captain Shaw said, lifting my chin the way Pa did when I was sad. "We'll all of us be a long time remembering."

"Did the cartridges arrive?" I asked. "Was the regiment able to reach the rebel lines?"

"Son, we didn't get more than a dozen men in the whole army onto the rebel works, and those few are likely prisoners. We got the cartridges, though, and they enabled us to withdraw from that rebel ambush."

"Calibre 54," I muttered.

"What did you say?" the captain asked.

"Calibre 54," I repeated. "Colonel Malmborg told me to be sure and bring calibre 54 ammunition."

"So that's what those Iowa boys meant," Captain Shaw said, laughing. "A whole company of them appeared, carrying boxes of cartridges. First thing they said was that they were sorry. They looked hard, but they couldn't find a single calibre 54 cartridge in the whole division."

"What?" I asked.

"Orry, do you even know what calibre 54 means?" Joe asked.

"It's the kind of ammunition, isn't it?" I replied.

"The size of ball," Captain Shaw explained. "Our Dresden rifles use calibre 58, or even calibre 57 cartridges, Orry. Thankfully, that's what the Iowans brought."

"You mean—"

"I suppose the colonel was a little rattled," Captain Shaw

said, shaking his head. "Maybe they used that 54-calibre ball when he was at military school in Sweden. Who knows? We sure wouldn't have found it much use to us."

"Then it was all for nothing," I said, closing my eyes a moment.

"For nothing?" the captain asked. "Who knows if anybody would have brought us ammunition if you hadn't gone to Sherman? He sent his aide over to find out if you were all right. You're the hero of the whole army, Orry."

"I don't feel much like one," I admitted. "My leg aches, and they're like as not to send me home now."

"No, we can't spare you," the captain insisted. "Heroes are hard to come by."

Epilogue

Orion Howe's wound was not serious, but it did keep him in a field hospital for several weeks. The Fifty-fifth Illinois made a second assault on the Confederate defenses on May 22, suffering five killed and fourteen wounded. That attack, like the ill-fated effort up the Graveyard Road, failed to breach the Vicksburg defenses. The Union commander, General Ulysses S. Grant, then laid siege to Vicksburg. After holding out for forty-seven days without reinforcement, with dwindling supplies of food and ammunition, the Southern commander, General John Pemberton, surrendered. Federal soldiers entered Vicksburg on July 4. The city did not again celebrate Independence Day for one hundred years.

That same week Union forces threw back the invading legions of Confederate General Robert E. Lee's Army of Northern Virginia at the small Pennsylvania town of Gettysburg. The Southern cause never recovered from the twin calamities.

Orion Howe celebrated the fall of Vicksburg at his grandmother's home. Colonel Malmborg had granted him a furlough on June 5, and Orion regained his strength under Roxanna Howe's watchful eye. He returned to the army in

August, but in November, Union General John Logan dispatched the "boy hero of Vicksburg" to Chicago for recruiting duty. On Christmas Day, 1863, Orion received a promotion to the rank of corporal. Thereafter he served as orderly for General Morgan L. Smith.

While he and his brother Lyston were delivering messages on horseback on May 28, 1864, Orion spied a group of Confederates advancing. He dismounted, took a rifled musket from a wounded comrade, and opened fire on the graycoats. The Confederates responded with a well-directed volley. Musket balls struck Orion twice in his right arm and once in the chest. With Lyston's help, Orion managed to escape. Fortunately, none of the wounds proved serious.

Orion was not yet finished with military life, though. General William T. Sherman, impressed by the boy's exploits at Vicksburg, had written the following letter to the United States Secretary of War, Edwin M. Stanton.

Headquarters Fifteenth Army Corps
Camp on Big Black, Aug. 8, 1863

Hon. E. M. Stanton, Secretary of War

Sir: I take the liberty of asking through you that something be done for a young lad named Orion P. Howe of Waukegan, Illinois, who belongs to the 55th Illinois, but is at present at his home, wounded. I think he is too young for West Point, but would be the very thing for a midshipman.

When the assault on Vicksburg was at its height, on the 19th of May, and I was in front near the road which formed my line of attack, this young lad came up to me wounded and bleeding, with a good healthy boy's cry: "General Sherman, send some cartridges to Colonel Malmborg; the men are all out." "What is the matter my boy?" "They shot me in the leg, sir; but I can go to the hospital. Send the cartridges right away!" Even where we stood the shot fell thick, and I told him to go to the rear at once, I would attend to the cartridges, and off he limped. Just before he disappeared, he turned and called as loud as he could, "Calibre 54!"

I have not seen the boy since, and his colonel, Malmborg, on inquiring, gave me his address as above, and says he is a bright, intelligent boy, with a fair preliminary education. What arrested my attention there was, and what renews my memory of the fact now is, that one so young, carrying a musket-ball wound through the leg, should have found his way to me at that fatal spot, and delivered his message, not forgetting the very important part even of the calibre of the musket, 54, which you know is an unusual one.

I'll warrant the boy has in him the elements of a man, and I commend him to the Government as one worthy of the fostering care of some one of its National Institutions.

I am, with respect, your obedient servant,
W. T. Sherman, maj.-gen, commanding.[1]

Stanton subsequently wrote the Navy Department, recommending Orion to them. The letter bears an endorsement by Abraham Lincoln. Orion's story spread. In September 1864 *Atlantic Monthly* carried George Boker's poetic description of Orion's heroism:

BEFORE VICKSBURG

May 19, 1863

While Sherman stood beneath the hottest fire
That from the lines of Vicksburg gleam'd,

---

[1]Committee of the Regiment, *The Story of the Fifty-fifth Regiment Illinois Volunteer Infantry in the Civil War, 1861–1865* (Clinton, Mass.: W. J. Coulter, 1887), 239.

And bomb-shells tumbled in their smoky gyre,
And grape shot hiss'd, and case shot scream'd,
     Back from the front there came,
     Weeping and sorely lame,
   The merest child, the youngest face,
Man ever saw in such a fearful place.

Stifling his tears, he limp'd his chief to meet;
But, when he paused and tottering stood,
   Around the circle of his little feet
There spread a pool of bright, young blood.
     Shocked at his doleful case,
     Sherman cried, "Halt! front face!
   Who are you? speak, my gallant boy!"
"A drummer, sir,—Fifty-fifth Illinois."

"Are you hit?" "That's nothing. Only send
   Some cartridges. Our men are out,
And the foe press us." "But, my little friend—"
   "Don't mind me! Did you hear that shout?
     What if our men be driven?
     Oh, for the love of Heaven,
   Send to my colonel, general dear—"
"But you?"—"Oh, I shall easily find the rear."

"I'll see to that," cried Sherman; and a drop,
   Angels might envy, dimm'd his eye,
As the boy, toiling towards the hill's hard top,
   Turn'd round, and, with his shrill child's cry
     Shouted, "Oh, don't forget!
     We'll win the battle yet!
   But let our soldiers have some more,
   More cartridges, sir, calibre fifty-four!"[2]

_____

[2]Ibid., 239–40.

Much was made of the request for .54 calibre ammunition. In recounting the incident in the regiment's official history, Lucien Crooker noted that the regiment's weapons were actually .58 calibre, and that when cartridges arrived, they proved to be .57 calibre, perfectly suitable for the Dresden model rifled musket.

Although Orion's service with the Fifty-fifth Illinois was relatively brief in comparison to many of the unit's other soldiers, he remained a favorite of both officers and men through and after the war. Orion received an appointment to the U.S. Naval Academy, passed the entrance examinations, and studied military science and navigation during the 1865–66 and 1866–67 terms. During his first year he performed well, but he amassed 236 demerits the following year, exceeding the number allowed a midshipman. Orion's crimes probably seemed minor to a boy who had faced Confederate muskets and cannons. While his former companions celebrated Lee's surrender, he was punished for skylarking at seamanship, appearing late at the mess hall, throwing books during study hours, and failing to take proper care writing in his journal.

Tired of the academy's discipline and eager to experience life at sea, Orion joined the merchant marine. Unfortunately his ship, the *Thornton*, wrecked off the coast of Ireland in November 1867. His close brush with death discouraged the young man, and he set off for the excitement of the "Wild West." As a civilian scout for the army, he was nearly killed by Modoc Indians at the Battle of the Lava Beds in January 1873. By 1877 he was in Parkville, Missouri, working as a saddle and harness maker.

Never one to ignore a challenge, Orion journeyed to Buffalo, New York, where he undertook the study of dentistry. Graduating, he returned to the West and built a modest practice in Sutton, Nebraska. When President Grover Cleveland extended to Civil War veteran regiments the opportunity to recognize their members for meritorious service, the Fifty-fifth Illinois Infantry submitted Orion Howe's name and the particulars of his heroism on the Graveyard Road. On April 23, 1897, the United States Government awarded its highest military decoration, the Medal of Honor, to Orion P. Howe, drummer and corporal. Orion received the decoration without ceremony or fanfare. It came in the mail.

Acknowledging the honor, Orion wrote, "to be thus distinguished is indeed an honor; though humbly deserved on my part is not less appreciated."[3]

Orion Howe lived a rich and full life. When he died on January 27, 1930, in Springfield, Missouri, friends and family gathered at the Klingner Funeral Home to mark the close of an extraordinary life. Today he rests in section 4, grave 207A, in the Springfield National Cemetery. His grave, together with those of four other Medal of Honor winners, is outlined in gold. On sunny days the headstone creates a remarkable impression.

Lyston D. Howe, who enlisted at age ten, was among the youngest soldiers to join the Union cause. He survived the war despite several serious bouts with illness. He completed his military service as orderly to General Giles A. Smith.

---

[3]U.S. National Archives Record Group 94 (AGO), Orion Howe Medal of Honor file.

Following his discharge in 1864, he visited Washington, D.C., where he finally had a chance to shake Abraham Lincoln's hand. Lyston died in Streater, Illinois, at age eighty-three.

Photo by G. Clifton Wisler

Of the remaining soldiers mentioned in these pages, Joe Edwards survived his shoulder wound. After three months in a Memphis hospital, he deserted while on leave in St. Louis in November 1863. He rejoined the regiment following a brief visit home; was wounded slightly at Kennesaw Mountain, Georgia, in June 1864; and was honorably discharged.

William H. Howe's military service left him plagued by rheumatism and other complaints. After struggling for two decades as a cabinet maker, he retired in July 1890 after convincing the federal government to grant him a twelve-dollar-per-month pension. Will Howe married a third time and was residing in Sioux City, Iowa, when he died on January 17, 1901.

Rienzi Cleveland won promotion to corporal in March 1864 but left the army at the expiration of his enlistment on October 31, 1864. Henry Woodring, Company C's good-humored giant, managed to escape rebel musket balls and the ravages of sickness until he also left the army in October 1864. Henry Curtiss and George Crowell died in the Fifty-fifth's reckless charge at Kennesaw Mountain on June 27, 1864. Sergeant John Curtiss fell a month later at Ezra Chapel. Colonel Oscar Malmborg never won the hearts of his men. Frustrated by repeated failure to win promotion, he cited declining health and his regiment's dwindling numbers in his letter of resignation, dated September 12, 1864. Milton Haney declined promotion to colonel in order to serve his companions as chaplain. His brother Richard was among those killed in the May 22 attack on Vicksburg's defenses.

Captain Francis Shaw briefly commanded the regiment at Kennesaw Mountain. On August 11, 1864, General Oliver Otis Howard dismissed Shaw from the service for "misbehavior before the enemy." A charge of cowardice was, and is, the most shameful mark any soldier can endure. Shaw, who had proved his valor at Shiloh, Vicksburg, and especially at Kennesaw Mountain, fought the charges. With the aid of his wartime compatriots, he persuaded the army to grant him an honorable discharge in 1887.

The Confederate soldiers imprisoned at Camp Douglas

were members of the Second Texas Infantry Regiment, a unit I know well. Hiram Bartlett died May 6 in prison. Following an exchange of prisoners, Will Stephens returned to his old regiment and again fought the Fifty-fifth Illinois Infantry at Chickasaw Bluffs and Vicksburg.

Author's Note

When I first happened upon the story of Orion Howe, I had already completed the daunting tasks of chasing two Civil War musicians, Ransom Powell and Willie Johnston, through the obscure pages of Civil War histories and down the narrow corridors of the U.S. National Archives. I had learned to comb census records, to examine pension papers, and to interpret the hen scratchings and abbreviated notes that haunt the compiled service records of Union soldiers serving in the Civil War. Orion was much better known than the other two. In fact, he was a hero in an age of heroes. It was a rare privilege to discover who he was and unravel his story.

Michael Musick, military historian at the U.S. National Archives in Washington, D.C., generously provided suggestions, pointed me to seldom-used documents, and answered questions. His name parted the waters of red tape and eased my quest.

I am equally indebted to Terry Winschel, historian at Vicksburg National Military Park. Although he was on temporary leave of absence when I visited the park, he kindly provided me material from the Vicksburg collection. Newspaper clippings given to Vicksburg by Shirley Barrett House and Franklin Barrett, descendants of Will Howe, shed light on some of the more confusing aspects of Orion's life.

Thanks to Ed Bearss, chief historian of the National Park Service, the rare and fragile history of the Fifty-fifth Illinois has been reprinted. I first obtained a copy through inter-library loan. The new edition includes photographs of Oscar Malmborg, Francis Shaw, and Orion P. Howe. In his fore-word, Bearss attributes his interest in the Fifty-fifth to an early effort to learn the story of the regiment's favorite hero.

In 1993, I participated in the Springfield Children's Lit-erature Conference in Missouri. Virginia Gleason and Sharol Higgins Neely of the Springfield–Greene County Library generously searched their collections for informa-tion about Orion Howe's later years. Although no journals or letters came to light, they located Orion's home; the records of his funeral; and death notices of Orion, his daughter Ella, and his son-in-law John Fulton. Visiting Springfield gave me the chance to view Orion Howe's grave and share the beginnings of this book with the school-children of southern Missouri.

Last, but certainly not least, I want to thank my sister-in-law, Melanie Drell Wisler, who served as my Illinois expert. I could not believe my luck when I discovered Company C was raised in her hometown of Rockford, Illinois.

About the Author

G. CLIFTON WISLER is the author of more than sixty books for children and adults. Among his titles are *Red Cap*, an ALA Best Book for Young Adults, and Golden Spur Award-winner *Thunder on the Tennessee*. An expert on the Civil War, Mr. Wisler stumbled across "the boy hero of Vicksburg" while doing research for his doctoral dissertation and decided that Orion Howe's life would make a terrific story.

A former junior high school English teacher, G. Clifton Wisler is now completing a doctorate in history at the University of North Texas. He lives in Plano, Texas.